She wanted to be with him.

"I kind of thought—" Shayla was suddenly shy. "You and I could go horseback riding. I packed a lunch."

Turner stared at her. "Well," he said, his heart hammering at a ridiculous rate, "I guess if you went to all the trouble of packing a lunch."

She burst out laughing.

And he realized it was funny. A grown man acting as though he found lunch irresistible, when it really was her.

He went to her in one long stride. He lifted her chin. Her eyes were huge, and her lips soft and moist. Calling his name, begging, though she spoke not a word.

"Maybe we're going too fast," he said softly.

"Too fast?" she whispered. "I thought there were no speed limits in Montana."

He kissed her then. Surrendering his hard-held control.

Completely.

Dear Reader,

In 20 months Silhouette Romance will celebrate its 20th anniversary! To commemorate that momentous occasion, we'd like to ask *you* to share with us why you've chosen to read the Romance series, and which authors you particularly enjoy. We hope to publish some of your thoughtful comments during our anniversary year—2000! And *this* month's selections will give you food for thought....

In *The Guardian's Bride* by Laurie Paige, our VIRGIN BRIDES title, a 20-year-old heiress sets out to marry her older, wealthy—gorgeous—guardian. Problem is, he thinks she's too young.... *The Cowboy, the Baby and the Bride-to-Be* is Cara Colter's newest book, where a shy beauty reunites a lonely cowboy with his baby nephew...and lassoes love in the process! Karen Rose Smith's new miniseries, DO YOU TAKE THIS STRANGER?, premieres with *Wealth, Power and a Proper Wife.* An all-work-and-no-play millionaire learns the value of his marriage vows when the wife he'd suspected of betraying him suffers a bout of amnesia.

Rounding out the month, we have *Her Best Man* by Christine Scott, part of the MEN! promotion, featuring a powerful tycoon who heroically offers protection to a struggling single mom. In *Honey of a Husband* by Laura Anthony, an ex-bull rider returns home to discover his childhood sweetheart is raising *his* child—by another woman. Finally, rising star Elizabeth Harbison returns to the lineup with *True Love Ranch,* where a city gal and a single-dad rancher lock horns—and live up to the Colorado spread's name.

Enjoy!

Joan Marlow Golan

Joan Marlow Golan
Senior Editor Silhouette Romance

Please address questions and book requests to:
Silhouette Reader Service
U.S.: 3010 Walden Ave., P.O. Box 1325, Buffalo, NY 14269
Canadian: P.O. Box 609, Fort Erie, Ont. L2A 5X3

THE COWBOY, THE BABY AND THE BRIDE-TO-BE

Cara Colter

Silhouette

ROMANCE™

Published by Silhouette Books

America's Publisher of Contemporary Romance

For Lynne Cormack,
my best friend
right through it all

SILHOUETTE BOOKS

ISBN 0-373-19319-X

THE COWBOY, THE BABY AND THE BRIDE-TO-BE

Copyright © 1998 by Cara Colter

Books by Cara Colter

Silhouette Romance

Dare To Dream #491
Baby in Blue #1161
Husband in Red #1243
The Cowboy, the Baby and the Bride-to-Be #1319

CARA COLTER

shares ten acres in the wild Kootenay region of British Columbia with the man of her dreams, three children, two horses, a cat with no tail and a golden retriever who answers best to "bad dog." She loves reading, writing and the woods in winter (no bears). She says life's delights include an automatic garage door opener and the skylight over the bed that allows her to see the stars at night.

She also says, "I have not lived a neat and tidy life, and used to envy those who did. Now I see my struggles as having given me a deep appreciation of life, and of love, that I hope I succeed in passing on through the stories that I tell."

Dear Nick,

I'm not a man too good with words. Or with babies, either. I can turn an honest day's work, though, and I'm a fair hand with a horse.

I guess I'm trying to tell you I'm a cowboy, plain and simple. I can face down a ton or so of raging, red-eyed Brahma bull without turning a hair. But babies—and women—scare the heck out of me.

The first time I saw you, I knew you belonged out on the ranch. You may be only three, but it was still there. In your eyes, in the way you stand, in the way you hold yourself.

Being a cowboy is more than puttin' on a hat and riding a bull. It's more than rodeos and wranglers. It's something in the soul.

Nicky, I don't want you growing up in the middle of a city, living in some cramped apartment, playing on concrete playgrounds. You're a boy who needs to run where there are no fences. You're a boy who needs to lasso sawhorse steers. You're a boy who needs to get bucked off old barrels rigged up with ropes.

How do I know? I look at you and see your daddy. And myself.

So I will teach you about this thing deep inside cowboys that needs blue skies and wide open spaces, that needs a good horse, and a herd of cattle, that needs to be strong.

And you will teach me about the most important thing of all.

Love. You will teach me about love.

Your uncle,

Turner

Chapter One

It was love at first sight.

Shayla had never used that expression before in her entire twenty-four years.

But then she had never seen anything like this before.

Montana.

The land was huge and breathtaking. Some people might have found the mile upon mile of treeless rolling plain desolate, but Shayla felt something in her opening up, soaring like that red-tailed hawk above her.

The prairie was in constant motion: the wind playing in tall golden grass, creating slow and sensuous waves; herds of pronghorns appearing in the distance, suddenly disappearing again; funny black-tipped spikes poking above the grass, turning out to be the ear tips of deer.

She unrolled the window on her ancient Volkswagen and took a deep breath of air that smelled of earth and sunshine, and something she couldn't quite define.

"Love at first sight," she repeated, out loud this time, letting it roll off her tongue.

"Bluv burst bite," her passenger echoed.

Shayla started. "Nicky! You're awake."

She turned and looked over her shoulder at her little charge, strapped securely in the brand-new car seat in the back of her car.

"Did you see them? The deer and antelope? It's just like the song," she realized with delight. "You know the one. 'Home, home on the range...'"

Nicky nodded solemnly, his eyes huge and black behind a sooty fringe of lashes. Dark loops of hair curled around his fat cheeks. He was a truly beautiful child, save for a tendency to beetle his brows and frown ferociously when he wanted his own way. Which was often.

"Me free," he said, holding up a fistful of fingers.

Free, she thought. That's what it was. The landscape spoke to something in her about wildness and freedom.

"That's right," she said, glancing at him in her rearview mirror. "Three." She noticed bright dots of color on each of his cheeks. "We're going to be at your uncle's soon. What do you think about that?"

"Me free."

She laughed. "Me, too. Having my first adventure at the ripe old age of twenty-four. Me, Shayla Morrison having an adventure!"

It wasn't really an adventure. She was doing a

friend a favor. That was all. But this landscape called out to a part of her that she hadn't known existed.

A part of her that longed for an adventure.

Tentatively she pushed her foot down a little harder. No speed limit in Montana. She had never gone fast in her whole life. The road was good, straight, paved and empty. Why not fly?

"Me six," Nicky announced.

"No, three."

In her rearview mirror, she watched black eyebrows drop down, and a pug nose scrunch up.

"Six!"

"It doesn't matter if you're three, when you're a tree," Shayla sang lightly, "and it doesn't matter if you are six if you are in a fix."

"Ohhh," Nicky breathed with delight. "Poppy Pepperseed."

Shayla laughed again. Her laughter felt rich within her, as glorious as this sun-filled day. For the past two years she had worked out of her home, writing the music and lyrics for the "Poppy Pepperseed Show," a locally-produced children's TV program in Portland, Oregon. Though she didn't do the voice or the singing for the program, Nicky invariably recognized when she became "Poppy."

"Sing," he commanded.

And so she sang. Nonsense lyrics that celebrated the huge sky and the circling hawks and the bouncing pronghorns. The next time she looked in the mirror her number-one fan was sound asleep.

She frowned. Again? How often did kids sleep? The red in his cheeks seemed to be deepening. He wasn't sick, was he?

She gave herself a little shake. She worried too much. Worrying was her specialty.

It was probably just boredom. They had been traveling now for two days.

A week ago, her neighbor Maria, a young single mom she had met about a year ago at the apartment's pool, had dropped Nicholas—Nicky—off for an afternoon as she occasionally did.

But by late that evening, the shy, beautiful Maria hadn't come back. Nicky had fallen asleep on the couch, his thumb in his mouth, cuddling his hand-knit purple-and-turquoise dinosaur, Ralph. It wasn't at all like Maria, who was soft-spoken and conscientious always, and Shayla began to wonder if she should start calling the hospitals.

When the phone rang, Shayla listened to the coins falling into place before Maria had come on the line.

"Shayla, I hate to ask, but could you keep Nicky for a day or two? Something has come up."

"Are you all right?" Shayla asked. Maria's voice sounded like it was coming from a long way away.

Maria laughed, and Shayla realized she had never heard her neighbor laugh before.

Of course she couldn't keep Nicky. He was not exactly the kind of child content to play on the floor with his Tonka toys while she plunked away at her old piano. Her next deadline was looming large.

"Please?"

A note in Maria's voice made her say yes. Her neighbor's voice held the smallest thread of happiness.

Maria always seemed to Shayla to be too young to look so tired and overburdened.

What was a day or two? She would have to figure out a way to work with Nicky around. Maybe even test the songs on him. A novel concept, testing a children's song on a real child.

What was a few days if it did something to take the sad and defeated slump out of Maria's thin shoulders?

Two days had come and gone, and then Maria had phoned again. She couldn't come back right away. Something had come up. An emergency. She wasn't sure when she would be back, actually, maybe weeks. Could Shayla take Nicky to his uncle in Montana?

That thread of happiness ran even stronger in Maria's voice.

"I can't go to Montana, Maria. When are you going to be back? What do you mean *weeks?*"

She knew she could not keep Nicky for weeks. He was a small tyrant, ordering her around like some tiny generalissimo dictator. No wonder Maria always looked so tired!

"Nicky eat. *Now.*"

"Nicky go to pool. *Now.*"

"Nicky not sleep. Nicky swim. *Now.*"

"Nicky not eat green. Nicky eat red. Lick-rish. *Now.*"

"Nicky playground. *Now.*"

Shayla was beginning to hear the word *now* in her sleep.

If her choice was to either keep him for weeks or take him to his uncle in Montana, she was going to Montana.

She had written down Maria's directions carefully and phoned in to work to tell them the music would be a little late. It was the first time in two years she had missed a deadline, but she was writing the Halloween episode, so she was nearly a month in advance of production, anyway.

As soon as she had started packing, she'd realized she felt happy.

"I think I wanted to get away," she murmured to herself, pressing down the accelerator just a little bit more. Seventy-two miles an hour. It was absolutely heady stuff.

Away from what?

Her job? It was true that after two years of writing the music for Poppy, her career was something less than challenging now. There were mornings she woke up and absolutely dreaded trying to think of a weather song, or a feelings song or any other kind of song that was going to be sung by adult actors dressed as puppets and furry animals...and clowns.

Which brought her to Barry Baxter. Bo-Bo the Clown on the show. Her beau-beau for the past year.

"You're going where?" he'd yelped when she'd called him. "Montana? With that kid?"

She'd resented the way he'd said that, as if Nicky was a two-headed monster instead of a child. A bossy child, yes, but still barely a baby nonetheless.

"You don't like kids, do you?" she'd asked with slow comprehension.

"It's not that I don't like them. I'm just surrounded by kid stuff all the time. The show, the kids who come on the show. I'm a man who wears a clown suit for a living. For Pete's sake when I take it off, I want to be a grown-up. No kids. And especially not that one."

"It's going to be that one for weeks, unless I go to Montana."

"Look, isn't there a law or something? She can't just dump her kid off there and expect you to deal with it."

"Are you suggesting I call the police? On sweet little Maria?"

"She's abandoned the kid."

"She has not."

Shayla sighed as she drove along. That was the real reason it felt so good to get away, she admitted to herself. She had a lot of thinking to do about herself and Barry.

Her mother thought she should marry him. So did Barry.

He was what her mother called a catch. Even though he was an actor, he had a steady job, and he was stable. He was also very good-looking, if just a trifle on the chubby side.

"You're never going to meet anyone else," her mother lamented. "You're a recluse, sitting at home plunking away on that piano. He's a nice boy. What's wrong with him?"

"There's nothing wrong with him," Shayla said desperately. "Is that a good reason to get married? Because there's nothing wrong with the person?"

"Shayla, this is your mother speaking. You marry a man with a good heart. A provider. Forget all these schoolgirl romantic notions. Forget your heart beating faster and skyrockets. There's nothing but pain in those things. I should know."

Shayla's mother and father had divorced years ago, a passion burned out quickly.

She had phoned to tell her mother she was going to Montana. How had the whole marriage issue come up?

"He doesn't like kids, Mom."

"There are worse things."

"I like kids."

"He loves you, Shayla. What more do you want?"

To love him back. She liked Barry. Her mother was right. She'd lived like a recluse until he'd come along. Now she had a charming companion to go to the movies with, to eat dinner with sometimes. They shared a certain creative bent that made them very compatible.

But marry him?

She didn't even really like kissing him. Why couldn't things just stay the same? Why did it have to move on? Why couldn't they just enjoy going to movies and out for dinner together?

But if she truly wanted things to stay the same how could she explain the creeping discontent she felt in a lot of areas of her life? She should like writing Poppy. She should feel lucky to have a job doing something in her field. With the exception of Lillian Morehouse, who was playing with the Philharmonic, ninety percent of her graduating class had not gained employment in the music field. Mike Webster's job in a record store didn't count.

It was Montana that was doing this to her—awakening some restless spirit within her, calling to some part of her that was just a touch wild and reckless.

Her mother and Barry had mournfully watched her pack the car to go.

"I can't believe you're doing something so hare-brained," Barry had said.

Her mother had nodded vigorous agreement.

Well, she'd hardly been able to believe it herself, but now that she was doing it, it felt great! Perhaps there had been a harebrained side of her, hidden for many years, just dying to get out.

She slowed, approaching an intersection, and glanced at the mileage covered, according to her trip meter. She had passed the small community of Winnet and the even smaller one of Sand Springs. This was it.

The signs were right beside the road, just as Maria had told her they would be.

Provided by the 4-H Club, neat placards said who lived down the road—the family name followed by the number of miles down that road.

Shayla scanned the placards quickly. There it was. MacLeod. Thirty-seven miles down that road. It looked like his closest neighbor was seven miles from him.

The immenseness of the country struck her anew. She got out, looked around, stretched and felt it again. Free.

Nicky slept on. She quietly opened the back door and loosened his little plaid shirt, so painstakingly stitched by his mother. The heat coming off him startled her.

It was a warm day, though, one of those September days that still held the full heat of summer.

When she got back in the car she unrolled the passenger-side window, too, so that the breeze could blow on Nicky.

She reset her trip meter and turned down the gravel road, somehow feeling her whole life was ahead of her.

At mile thirty-seven there was a big-timbered gatepost that spanned a drive on the west side of the road. Hanging from the weathered center beam was a piece of driftwood with the name MacLeod burned deep into it. In this barren country, where only a few spindly deciduous trees grew in the draws, it must have taken quite a bit of effort to get those timbers.

She drove under the sign. She had expected to see a house, but instead it was another road, more narrow now, twisting and dipping over little rolls of land and through small coulees.

She had gone another five miles before she topped a rise in the undulating landscape and saw the buildings sprawled out in the draw below her.

She stopped the car and checked Nicky. He was still sleeping soundly, his cheeks, thankfully, felt cooler to her now.

She looked down at the buildings below her. It wasn't much, really. A small square of a house, a barn that looked newer and more distinguished than the house, and a few scattered outbuildings.

A cloud of dust drew her eyes beyond the outbuildings to a corral. She shielded her eyes against the sun.

"Oh, my," she whispered.

A man stood dead center in that corral, while a beautiful black horse galloped around him, kicking and bucking.

Even from a distance she could see he was the quintessential cowboy. Whipcord lean in his dust-covered jeans, denim shirt, a big-brimmed white cowboy hat shading him from the sun. She liked the way he was standing, loose-limbed and calm in the middle of all that ruckus, radiating an easy strength.

And then he took off the hat and wiped a careless sleeve over a sweating brow.

Even from a distance his features seemed even and clean, pleasing to the eye.

Her heart somersaulted, and again she used an expression she had never used until today.

''Love at first sight.''

She blushed at her own silliness.

The man was a stranger, glimpsed from a distance. He did make a decidedly romantic figure, but obviously Montana had had a strange effect on her senses—heightened and honed them to a dangerous sharpness.

If she had an ounce of sense, she would get back in her car and go down the road the way she'd come.

But then if she had an ounce of sense, as Barry and her mother had already told her, she wouldn't be here in the first place.

She'd made a commitment to deliver Nicky to his uncle, and she would carry it through until the end.

She got back in her car and pointed it right toward those buildings.

The dust behind the car must have told him she was coming. As she pulled up to the house, he was in the yard, if not waiting for her, at least done working the horse for a moment.

He was sitting on the edge of a water barrel in front of his house, one foot anchoring him on the ground, a dipper in his hand. His hat was on the stoop beside him. His hair was thick, the rich color of melted chocolate. He took a slow swallow of water, watching her over the edge of the dipper.

When she drew to a halt, he saluted her mildly, hung the dipper from a nail on the wall, retrieved his hat and, tugging it down over his brow, stood and came toward the car.

For a minute she was absolutely frozen where she was.

He had the lean grace of a cowboy as he moved toward her, one-hundred-percent man.

Not that Barry wasn't one-hundred-percent man, but it was a different kind of percentage.

He was smiling, a warm smile that showed beautiful teeth and crinkles around his eyes.

Eyes a color she had seen only once before. Last night. Just before the sun had gone down, the sky had turned the most incredible shade of blue. Indigo, really.

And he was smiling at her, hypnotizing her with incredible indigo eyes.

She stumbled out of the car.

"Ma'am," he said, touching the brim of his hat.

She commanded herself to look way up at him, break the spell of those eyes, but she absolutely couldn't. He was stunning.

She was suddenly aware how rumpled she must look after two days on the road. She wished she'd thought to comb her hair when she'd paused up there on the knoll—applied a little lipstick. And mascara. Eye shadow. Hair dye.

Anything so that it wasn't plain-Jane Shayla Morrison standing there with the most spectacular man she had ever seen.

"Are you lost?" he asked, his eyes flicking from her to the car, resting for a moment, warmly, on the little bundle snoozing in the back seat.

She was lost all right, and she'd better pull out before she went any farther into the depths of those astounding eyes.

"I've brought you your nephew," she blurted out.

Even before she registered the surprise in his features it occurred to her something was wrong. He should have been expecting her.

"His mother said you would be expecting me." Her voice trembled. She'd come so far. How on earth could this be happening? She suddenly felt exhausted and confused.

Her mother and Barry had been right. What a harebrained thing to do. Now what was she going to do?

"You must have taken a wrong turn somewhere, ma'am. It's easy enough to do in this country. I don't have a nephew. One niece."

His voice was slow and easy, deep and wonderful. How could he say a word as proper as *ma'am* and make her feel as if he'd said something deliciously indecent? How could he say something that made her feel deliciously indecent and reassured at the same time?

He didn't have a nephew, but it was just a wrong turn.

"Wrong turn," she stammered. "Of course, you must be right. I must have—" she thought of the big sign over the front gate "—I must have found the wrong MacLeod. Is there another one?" She felt flustered as the amusement leaped in his eyes.

"Lots of MacLeods in this country. Which one are you looking for?"

Nicky suddenly let loose a holler from the backseat, like a cat with its toenail caught in the screen door.

"Turner," she said, pivoting from him, bending into the car to release the belt on the car seat. "I'm looking for Turner MacLeod."

She looked back. His jaw had dropped. It was a strong jaw, deeply shadowed.

"Well, that would be me, ma'am, but I don't—"

Nicky exploded from his seat and pushed by her. He ran straight for the big lean man who was eyeing them now with horrified fascination.

Nicky grabbed Turner MacLeod's blue jeans in a tight chubby fist. His head dropped. He threw up on the man's boots.

Shayla closed her eyes in mortification. Thousands of miles of open prairie, and Nicky had chosen the man's boot? Barry would have been furious.

"Oh," she said, "I'm so sorry."

Nicky was shrieking, still holding that leg.

The man squatted down, ignoring the substance on his boot. He took Nicky's tiny shoulders in both strong hands and scanned his face, and then touched his forehead quickly with the back of his hand.

Turner scooped up the boy with easy strength, tucked him into his shoulder. "Better come in. He's got a bit of a fever."

The calm in his voice quelled the panic in the pit of her stomach.

She froze, looking at them together. Nicholas's coloring was different from Turner's, darker and more exotic, but the bone structure was identical.

She had the sudden sinking sensation that Maria had not sent her to the boy's uncle after all.

Turner MacLeod was Nicholas's father.

And he didn't know it.

Love at first sight and he was an utter cad.

She could almost see her mother sniffing triumphantly. Hear her voice in her mind saying, "Don't you trust hormones or hearts to make those really important decisions, Shayla. This is your mother talking. Use your head. That's what the good Lord gave it to you for."

Well, her head was saying run, and run fast. But her feet were following his long stride toward his porch. She couldn't very well leave Nicky here with a perfect stranger. Even if it was his father.

"I better get him to a hospital," she said frantically.

He shot her a quick look over his shoulder. "Ma'am, the nearest hospital is a long, long way from here."

He said it quietly, patiently, even, but she could sense a judgment, and a harsh one. Outsider. City slicker. Not aware of the realities of life in these big empty spaces.

He slipped off his boots at a jack on the porch outside his screen door. Then he opened the door and held it with a foot, indicating for her to follow him.

"I don't even know you," she said, hesitating.

He shot her an incredulous look. "You might have thought of that a couple of hundred miles ago." The door squeaked and closed behind him.

"How do you know how far I've come?" She suddenly felt even more suspicious. Oh great, she had driven hundreds of miles to walk straight into the clutches of the only ax murderer in Montana.

"The license plates say Oregon, ma'am. That's one hell of a pile of time to give some thought to what you're doing."

"Back then I thought you knew Nicky!"

"Nicky," he repeated it slowly. He held the caterwauling boy back, and studied his face.

Nicky was making a lot of noise but not crying. Shayla had noticed the little boy had a particularly tough streak in him. He *never* cried.

A light came on in Turner MacLeod's face as he studied the boy. A light, followed by a look of bewildered tenderness that completely erased her worries about the position of the nearest ax.

"Geez," he breathed under his breath. He looked up at her, his eyes pinning her with intense blue light. "Who's his mama?"

Just how many beds had his boots been under? she wondered, borrowing a phrase from a song she wished she had written.

"Maria Gerrardi," she said tightly. She added silently—a good Catholic girl, whose life lies in ruins because of you, you handsome devil you.

Something tightened in his features.

With another look at Nicky's face, he sighed and disappeared into the darkness of his house.

Chapter Two

She was standing out on his porch deciding whether or not it was safe to come in, he thought wryly.

She was probably from a big city—an alarm on her key chain, a half dozen dead bolts on her doors, a penchant for watching evening news that scared her silly.

She probably thought he had an ax in here.

He set the boy down on a chair. "Stay," he said sternly.

The little boy continued caterwauling, but looked at him with huge startled eyes. Turner noticed, for all the noise, the kid was dry-eyed.

He had eyes, huge and coal dark, just like Turner's brother, Nicholas. Even the same name. Nick. A strange coincidence that the boy was here now. He hadn't seen Nick for nearly four years. And then a couple of days ago the satellite dish had decided to work, and he'd caught the tail end of the news when they did the human interest stuff.

And there was Nick, in a park uniform, talking about grizzly bears and living alone on some godforsaken mountain, studying them.

The reporter, a pert little blond in a miniskirt, asked the typical question of a hermit. "Don't you crave human company?"

If Turner wasn't mistaken, there might have been just a hint of invitation in the question to his handsome brother.

"Only one," Nick had said slowly, missing the invitation. "And I lost her a long time ago. I've learned something on this mountain. If you want something with your whole heart and soul, don't listen when other people try to tell you it doesn't make sense, don't listen when they tell you no."

Of course, *he'd* been the SOB who told his little brother no to Maria Gerrardi.

Though, from the look of this young pup in front of him, he hadn't said no quite soon enough.

The interview had opened old wounds. Made him wish he'd done some things differently, made him wish you could go back and try it again. Only with more patience and wisdom—the patience and wisdom that the painful estrangement from his brother had given him.

Turner had been seventeen years old when he was thrust into a man's world, had had to shoulder a man's responsibilities. His parents had been killed when their private plane crashed, leaving him to cope with a huge ranch and two younger siblings.

It had been scary and hard. The scary part he never showed, and the hard part he got too good at. He'd been so busy trying to keep everything together, trying to keep Nick and Abby out of trouble, that he hadn't noticed he wasn't exactly communicating with them.

And if he had noticed, he probably wouldn't have known how to change it, anyway. Seventeen. What do seventeen-year-olds know about communicating?

Taking charge. Taking control. Snapping orders. That's what he'd gotten good at. Too good.

When Nick left he'd shouted angrily at Turner, "No one's even allowed to breathe around here without your say-so."

The words still stung.

But now this. His brother's son here. Did that mean he was going to get a second chance? Was he so much better at communicating now, that he could say, "Nick, it was always for love." He'd wanted the best for them. For his brother and sister.

Abby knew. But Nick had decided grizzly bears were better than an overbearing brother. *Who had meant well.* Why hadn't that part come through?

He sighed. Probably because of Maria. Nick had just finished college. He'd been way too young. He had his whole life ahead of him.

But Turner hadn't said it like that at all. And when Nick had shown every sign of not listening, Turner had taken it upon himself to go talk to Maria. She'd listened. She'd been gone the next day. And a look as black as the devil's heart had come into Nick's eyes and never gone away. After a month of treating Turner to looks snapping with ill-concealed anger, he'd accepted a job at a remote mountain wilderness park.

Turner had thought he would last a month. He'd

been wrong. He didn't like it one bit that his brother matched him for stiff-necked stubbornness.

Why had Maria sent the boy here?

He felt sick when he thought of her crying that night, four years ago. Saying she understood. She wasn't good enough for his brother…she'd always known that. At the time, Turner had been sure he was doing the right thing, arranging everybody's lives to his own satisfaction.

Four years without so much as a Christmas card from his brother. A hell of a price to pay for being right. And now, finding out a child had lived without his daddy because he'd been so sure he was right.

Things were about to happen big-time. He could practically sniff it in the air, the same way he could smell a big storm rolling in.

The wee Nicky, built like a sturdy little dump truck, stopped howling. That must have convinced her it was safe, or that she needed to attempt a rescue, but either way the door squeaked open and she came in.

She stood hesitantly inside the door, the light framing her. She was slender and willowy, and despite the jeans and T-shirt, she reminded him of a ballerina he'd seen at the ballet Celia had dragged him to. He'd slept through most of the damned thing, but he remembered that ballerina, looking so fragile and dainty, hiding incredible strength.

"Aspirin's over the stove," he told her. "Grab it, would you?"

"I read somewhere you shouldn't give aspirin to babies because—"

"Look, lady, the nearest drugstore is a pretty long

haul, okay? Nearly as far as the hospital. We make do out here.''

He reached into the fridge. A carton of apple juice happened to be among the isolated inhabitants. He grabbed it and slammed the door quick before she caught sight of that plate of blue-green something that he had at one time planned to reheat.

He wondered, briefly, why he cared if she caught sight of the molding contents of his fridge.

''Oh,'' she said, from across the room, ''this isn't aspirin. It's acetaminophen. That's okay then.''

''Could you crush whatever it is and bring it here?''

Acetaminophen. It was all aspirin to him. He slid her a look.

There was certainly nothing glamorous about his unexpected visitor. She had no high-gloss hairdo, the kind that stayed perfectly in place even when the wind picked up, which it did plenty around here. The sun was shining through her hair right now. Outside, it had looked plain, old light brown. In here it looked like liquid honey, curling around her neck and ending just before her shoulders.

But anybody who called aspirin acetaminophen with such ease probably had taken in a ballet or two herself. And not slept through it, either.

If he was shopping for a woman, which of course he wasn't, he needed one who wore cowboy boots, not one with painted toenails and flimsy shoes.

He did a quick check. Sandals. Little pink dots on each toe. Cute toes, now that he looked. But no doubt she would be all lace and silk under the plain old T-shirt and jeans she was wearing.

Now what had made him think of that? And why did that quick mental flash make his mouth go dry as if he was stuck in a sandstorm?

Maybe it was the way those jeans had clung in all the right places when she had bent into the car to release the catch on the car seat, and then again when she had stretched up to that cabinet above the fridge.

"What's the holdup?" Turner growled.

"It's harder than you think!"

He moved across the kitchen to her, painfully aware suddenly of what a plain room it was. The linoleum was old and worn. The table was a relic from an old bunkhouse. There were only two chairs, one with a plastic seat that had been patched with hockey tape and another with three different colors of paint showing through the worn spots. Well, he hadn't been expecting highfalutin' company. At least the place was clean. He'd learned to keep up with housework long ago the hard way. Rinsing a dish right after he ate was a lot easier than trying to blowtorch month-old remains off of them.

He looked over her shoulder. He couldn't help but notice the top of her head came up to about the bottom of his chin. And that she smelled good. Of soap and shampoo and something sweet and tantalizing that was pure woman.

She was trying to beat the aspirin to death with a soup ladle.

He took two spoons out of his kitchen drawer, placed a tablet between them and squeezed. Instant powder.

"This is how you squish *acetaminophen*." He

mixed the powder in a teaspoon of apple juice, went back across his kitchen and spooned it into the kid.

The kid spit it out on him.

"Little man, you sure do know how to make a first impression. Squish me another one of those, would you?"

He got up and found some tea towels, ran them under lukewarm water in the sink. "Running water," he said. "Had it for near six months now." He drawled it out nice and slow like a real hick. He kept his face completely deadpan.

She cast him a sideways look from under lashes that he noticed were as thick and tangled as a sooty chimney brush. It didn't look like she had mascara on though, or any other war paint, either. No bright red lips or stripes of green over her eyes. No little pencil-thin eyebrows or slashes of fake pink on her cheeks.

He didn't revise his first opinion. She was no beauty. But there was something just plain natural about her that was easy on a man's eyes. He decided he'd had nothing to look at but horses for a sight too long.

She was grunting trying to squish the tablets. Not enough muscle in those arms to wring out a dishrag. If he was shopping for a woman, which of course he wasn't, he needed one who could heft a bale or two.

She wasn't Celia, he realized suddenly, and it wasn't fair to her to treat her like she was, or to assume that all women from the cities would be the same. Maybe she wasn't even from a city.

"Which part of Oregon are you from?" he asked.

"Portland."

Best to keep his guard up. Celia, a born-and-bred Baltimore girl, had thought the country would be romantic as all get-out, and she'd had a notion or two about cowboys, too. All of them wrong.

She had thought Turner was rugged and real because she'd seen him ride to glory for eight seconds on the back of a raging bull.

As long as he was handing his Stetson to maître d's or the hatcheck girl at the ballet her illusions were pretty safe.

Then he'd made the mistake of asking her out here.

Her disappointment and disillusionment had set almost at once. Her first impression of this very room had put a look on her face that would have soured milk.

Then his best reining horse had foaled badly, and the foal had ended up behind the heater in the house, with him trying to coax an eyedropper of milk into it about every ten seconds or so.

It had pretty much sealed his fate when he didn't even have a candle to light for the special dinner she'd made him. He'd offered to drive over to his sister's—an hour-and-five-minute round trip—but the moment was definitely lost. She'd said it didn't matter. When he'd seen those escargot things in full light he'd wished he'd insisted on making the trip.

Turner knew it was for the best, her leaving. They'd been living in some sort of fantasy world, and the reality check had been inevitable. The truth was out. *Rugged and real* meant he was hardworking, stubborn, a loner, and about as romantic as a skunk in a trap.

He'd wondered so much about whether or not those

candles really had mattered that on his next grocery run to town he'd picked up a pair of nice red ones, and bought three videos. For next time.

So far there hadn't been a next time. The candles were still wrapped and so were the videos.

Maybe his unexpected guest would be impressed. Since the videos were now three years old he doubted it.

He hadn't been to a rodeo in nearly that long, either. He was getting old, he supposed. At thirty, a ton of Brahma bull, tap dancing on his chest, was not as appealing as it had been a decade ago.

He liked working with horses. He'd finalized an arrangement with his sister and his brother-in-law just last year where they would run the cattle part of the ranch that had been in his family since shortly after Noah, and he could devote himself to doing what he did best. He'd bought this little parcel over here because he liked the barn.

He was a good trainer and he knew it. He had more business than he could handle. Between his training fees, selling colts he'd finished, and his share of the profits from the ranch, he made a pretty fine living. He would actually have lots of money, if he could ever learn to curb his impulse to buy just one more horse.

Turner had paid seven thousand dollars for the lunatic Appaloosa out there. His sister had sighed, looked at his house and had the good sense to say nothing.

Horses made him happy. Show him a house that could do that.

Life was good. Settled. All right, he missed his

brother. And from time to time he yearned for the soft company of a pretty woman.

A man got lonely. There was nothing that brought out his vulnerability like this time of year, the promise of winter already in the air at night, the thought of short days and long cold nights filling him with an ache he didn't want to feel.

He'd wanted very badly for it to work with Celia. But it hadn't, and it had killed something in him trying to make it. Having a woman digging her spikes into the region near your heart was no less painful than the bull tap dancing. He was too old for them both.

There wasn't an available woman within a thousand square miles. He knew all the girls, long since turned into women, who had grown up around here, and they were either long gone or long taken. And he was too proud and stubborn and busy to go searching worlds unfamiliar to him like some lonely-hearts-club reject.

But this one had come to him.

Turner slid a glance to her ring finger. Blank. He was aware, suddenly, of a sense of something missing from his life since he'd given up rodeo.

Adventure. Spontaneity. Not knowing precisely what was going to happen next.

Geez, MacLeod, he told himself. Don't go bein' no fool. He noticed a little scattering of light freckles over her nose.

She finally managed to break up the acetaminophen.

"You try and give it to him this time," he said

gruffly. "Then we'll get his clothes off and sponge him down real good."

She took the juice from him and sat down across from the little boy who looked at her with mulish stubbornness that reminded him of his own brother.

"Oh, little love, open wide," she sang in such a clear true voice it made Turner start, "let this magic come inside, chase away all the germs that hide—"

The little scoundrel opened his mouth like a baby bird, and swallowed the medicine with a satisfied slurp.

"Did you just make that up, just now?" Turner asked incredulously.

"Oh," she said with a self-conscious laugh. "It's silly, but it works."

Her eyes crinkled up at the edges when she laughed, and they were a nice color. Hazel, he supposed it was called, when they were kind of gold and green and brown all mixed together like that.

"Sing again, Poppy. *Now.*"

"No," she said uncomfortably, a sudden blush painting her high cheekbones a becoming shade of scarlet.

Poppy. Despite the color in her cheeks at the moment, it didn't suit her. Poppies, in his mind, were flamboyant flowers, in too-brilliant shades of red or orange.

She was more like a little brown-eyed Susan.

"Go ahead," he said. "I liked it." More than liked it. It was like listening to an angel sing.

But she wouldn't sing again. Instead she took off the little boy's shirt and sponged him off with those tea towels he'd prepared.

"Let's lay him down," he suggested. "The back room stays cool."

When she moved to lift the boy, he took him from her.

"He's not heavy," she protested.

He shrugged. Oh, right. It was this brand-new world where women did all the same things as men. Never mind that he had just been evaluating her bale-throwing ability. He suspected it was this kind of thing that had driven Nick away—he demanded the best from everyone and then never gave them a chance to show it to him. But other than toss the kid back at her, he didn't know what to do about it.

They went down the narrow hall. He managed to snag his bedroom door with his toe on the way by and pull it shut before she got a glimpse of three or four days' worth of dirty shirts and socks on the floor.

His spare bedroom was as plain as the rest of his tiny house. It didn't even have a curtain. Not many Peeping Toms could be bothered coming out this far.

Especially to only get a peep at him.

"Poppy, sing," the wee tyrant demanded again as she tucked relatively clean sheets around the tyke.

She glanced self-consciously in Turner's direction, and he took the hint and left. He had a pair of boots that needed cleaning before they were ruined, anyway.

But as he bent over the boots with the garden hose, he could hear her voice drifting out the window.

"Oh, little love, close your eyes,
Think of sun and wide blue skies,

Deer playing and grass swaying,
Coyotes at the moon baying..."

After a few minutes the singing stopped. He realized he had stood there, frozen, not paying the least bit of attention to his boots.

She came out the back door a moment later. "He went right to sleep."

"How do you do that? Just make up rhymes to music like that?"

"I don't know. It just comes to me. I'm sorry about your boots."

"They've seen worse."

"What could be worse?" she asked, crinkling up her nose.

He decided to be a gentleman and not describe to her in generous detail the afterbirth of a cow.

"Should we call a doctor?" she asked. "Maybe just run Nicky's symptoms by him?"

"We'll wait and see. I don't think it's much. Could be too much heat. Maybe he's carsick. I think the temperature will come right down now."

"You handle a crisis very well."

He snorted. "This is a long way from a crisis. But when you do have a crisis, you don't have any choice when you're this far from anything."

She hugged herself and looked out over the land. "I think this is right in the middle of everything."

Sure you do, honey. "Until the first time you crave pizza at two in the morning."

"Pizza is easy to make."

"It is?" he said with reluctant respect.

"Oh, sure. A little bread dough and tomato sauce, pepperoni, and fresh green peppers."

"Fresh. There you have it. What we don't have."

"I can eat it without," she said absently. "You could grow a garden, couldn't you?"

He shot a guilty look at the dead flowers in the box under the bedroom window.

She followed his gaze. "Oh. Did you plant those?"

"Not hardly," he said a trifle defensively. Did he look like the kind of man who planted pansies?

Something tightened in her face, and he could read the whole story of what she thought had happened there. He'd had a brief fling with a woman who thought she was staying and had planted flowers. He'd gotten rid of her and not even bothered to water the plants.

Actually, his sister had planted the flowers in one of those periodic attempts she made to spiff his place up. He'd watered them meticulously for a week or so. And then he'd gotten contracts to put thirty days' training on six horses, plus he'd acquired that renegade, leopard-spotted Appy mare who only had murder—his—on her mind.

He decided, stubbornly, not to tell his uninvited guest those few facts, even if they might have redeemed his hardened soul somewhat in her eyes.

If she was silly enough to think he was some kind of playboy, let her think it. It might keep her from getting any damn fool notions.

That kid was going to be here for a day or two, and she wasn't leaving without him tucked in his little seat in the back of her little car.

"Poppy, is it?" Perhaps that would explain a sensitivity to perished flowers.

She looked baffled.

"Your name?"

"Good grief, no. Shayla. Shayla Morrison."

He thought Poppy was a somewhat more sensible name, even if it didn't suit her. Shayla was an exotic name, which for some ridiculous reason made him wonder about her underwear again. Frills. He'd bet his last buck on that one. Come to that, he'd probably bet his soul for one little peek, so he'd better get himself out of harm's way and quick.

"Miss Morrison—"

"Shayla, please."

"Shayla, I've got some chores to do, so you've got the place to yourself if you want to have a bath or shower. I'll pull out the sofa bed for the night."

"I can't stay here!"

"Well, you sure as hell can't leave. That kid isn't going anywhere, and you're not going anywhere without him."

She mulled that over. "And the nearest motel?"

"Care to guess?"

"Close to the pharmacy and hospital?"

"Right around the corner."

"I guess you're right."

"An irritating habit I have."

She smiled, and it was a nice smile that showed small white teeth and lit up a light inside her eyes, making him realize he'd been wrong about one thing. Because she was downright beautiful when she did that.

The smile disappeared, and she gnawed on her bottom lip thoughtfully. "I don't know what I'm going to do—"

"I think you're going to have to stick around. For

a day or two. I'll see if I can track down Maria and find out what's going on.''

''Track her down? But—''

''She used to have some family in these parts.'' Family, he remembered, who lived in a frightful little shack with a car corpse or two in the yard. Part of the reason he'd decided she was completely unsuitable for his brother.

MacLeod, he told himself, *you're a real SOB.*

''I'm sure she's planning to call you,'' Shayla said. ''I can stay the night, but—''

''You can't leave him here. You either have to stay or take him with you when you go. He strikes me as a tough little tyke, but his Mom's gone, and I think he'd be scared to death if you dropped him here with a complete stranger.''

The depth of his caring for the little boy took him slightly aback.

''I think you're right,'' she said, apparently as surprised by his sensitivity as he himself was.

''Are you rushing back to a job or a boyfriend or something?''

''Not really. I can do my job anywhere.''

''What job is that?'' No mention of a boyfriend? Why did that make his stupid heart skip a beat?

''I write songs for a children's show.''

''That explains it. The songs you pull out of the air.'' For some reason her offbeat job made her seem appealing.

Then again after three years without so much as a kiss, he'd probably see appeal in just about anyone, up to and including Ma Baker who ran a pretty good café in Jordan—and was two hundred and thirteen pounds, and damn proud of every one of them.

And now he'd gone and encouraged her to stay. Sleep in his bed. Take a shower. She'd get out all rosy and smelling of sweetness and soap—

And he'd work himself into the ground until well after dark, come in, hit the sack and fall into a deep, dreamless and exhausted sleep. He could manage that for a day or two. Actually it wouldn't be that different from his regular routine.

He watched her go into the house, and he pulled on his newly cleaned boots.

He noticed the door to her car was still open and went to give it a shove before her battery died.

Her suitcase was still in the back seat.

He hesitated. He'd told her she'd have the place to herself, but all her clean clothes were out here. It wouldn't hurt him to do the gentlemanly thing before he vamoosed down to the corral for a session with that hell-horse.

The one he wasn't getting paid to work with, he reminded himself with a wry shake of his head.

He picked her suitcase out of the back seat.

It was old and battered, not like those Gucci bags of Celia's.

He took the steps two at a time and went into the house. He was crossing the living room, when without warning the top flap flew open and her possessions scattered across his living room floor.

He said a word he generally didn't say within hearing distance of women and children.

Who generally weren't within hearing distance of him.

He bent and began to cram things back into the suitcase. He was trying hard not to look, but there wasn't a scrap of lace or silk in the whole works.

Plain old white cotton.

What he felt for her at this moment was the oddest thing. A pretty little woman like that without one pretty little thing. He felt strangely sad for her.

Right from the start he'd known she was the kind of woman who should have silk and lace. He was pretty sure there was passion there, right below that calm surface—

"Oh!"

She had come down the hallway, and was standing there looking at him shoving her personal stuff back into her bag.

"Sorry," he mumbled. "The catch—"

"I know," she said. "Broken."

He glanced up at her. She was blushing. Well, unless he was mistaken, so was he.

She came quickly toward him. "Here. That's all right. Let me."

She squatted beside him. Her hand touched his in a frantic effort to get to a white unmentionable before he did.

Her skin was as soft as that silk he'd just been thinking of, and a jolt went through him like he'd been hit full-strength with a cattle prod.

He scrambled to his feet. "I've got horses to see to."

"Would you like me to make dinner?"

Dinner. Dinner. "Sure. When you're hungry. Help yourself."

"I meant for you."

"Dinner for me?" He gawked at her.

"I don't mind. I certainly don't expect you to cook for Nicky and me."

"You won't find anything much to make it with. I think I've got some tins of stew and wieners and beans. Frozen dinners in the freezer."

She smiled. "I'll see what I can do."

Now he wasn't going to be able to hide in the barn until all the lights went off in the house. He was going to have to sit across from her and have dinner and think of things to say.

It had been a long time.

And suddenly he was looking forward to it.

In for a penny, in for a pound, he thought. "You'll find some red candles over there in that drawer."

He turned abruptly on his heel and left her there neatly folding things back into her suitcase.

Lordy, he was in big trouble. Thank God he had horses waiting—one waiting to kill him.

And with any luck it would do precisely that before he ever found out how big the trouble really was that he was in.

Chapter Three

She was staying. In the home of a complete stranger. A dangerously attractive complete stranger. For one night and maybe two.

It was absurd. Crazy.

Why was she so happy about it?

Because her heart *liked* him. Her head didn't. Her head was full of her mother's voice telling her to beware. Reminding her Turner might be Nicky's father, not his uncle.

But her heart held tight to the warmth she had seen in his gaze when he first looked at Nicky, to his lack of concern over the condition of his boots after Nicky's unfortunate accident on them, and to his very real concern for a sick child.

That alone, she told herself, had earned him the pizza she was making him for supper.

His cupboards were quite well supplied with dry goods, though most of the good stuff was way at the back, behind the rows of canned stew, spaghetti and ravioli. She found tomato sauce and tiny tinned sausages and biscuit mix.

His fridge contained a six-pack of soda pop, a twenty-pound bag of apples, a ten-pound bag of carrots, some strange blue-green substance busily growing fur and two small blocks of cheese.

Not an onion or green pepper to be seen.

When everything was ready she set it on top of the oven. She'd wait until he came in.

She checked on Nicky, relieved that he was now cool and breathing easily.

She smiled at the spartan, tidy little room.

His world, Turner's world, was obviously not within the confines of these four walls. His world was out there—the rough and rugged world she had first seem him in, standing in the center of a dusty corral as some half-wild horse lunged around him.

She lugged her traitorous suitcase down the hall and took a shower, berating herself for not having had the latch fixed and wishing she owned some frothy underwear.

It had been awful seeing his big tanned hands cramming her most personal things back into that suitcase.

Especially since her most personal things were so ordinary.

Everything she owned was ordinary, she thought, getting out of the shower and fishing through each item in her suitcase with a critical eye.

She finally settled for mossy green jeans and a matching cream-coloured flannel shirt with a faint green stripe. She tied her damp hair back with an elastic and made a face at herself in the smoky mirror. She wasn't trying to make herself attractive for *him*, was she? She decided, perhaps a little more emphatically than necessary, that she was not. She was a guest in his home, and it was only decent that she make herself neat and presentable.

She had long ago accepted she was not one of those women who was ever going to turn a head as she walked down the street. Construction workers did not whistle at her. Teenage boys did not crane their necks or drive their bicycles into the backs of cars to get a better look.

She had neat and tidy features, ordinary really.

Her university days had been largely without the rush of romance. She'd been dedicated to her studies, and quite shy. She chose the study carrels at the library rather than the open tables. She had developed some very solid friendships with both sexes, but an actual relationship evaded her.

Her mother, who seemed to consider university a happy hunting ground for the unwed, found her lack of romantic involvement with some budding doctor or lawyer very discouraging.

Her mother's distress had increased when Shayla found a job where she would be working mostly out of her own apartment rather than where she would be meeting people—make that "men"—of interest.

Did part of her actually delight in thwarting her mother's plans for her?

Is that why her wardrobe was minus form-hugging shirts in siren red, or lace-trimmed blouses that would make her look wonderfully feminine and alluring?

She had met Barry while delivering music to the

small cable station where the show was produced. It wasn't her appearance that had attracted him. She remembered the startled appreciation on his face when one of the songs she had written for Bo-Bo that week made him laugh. He'd asked her out for lunch. She'd been her usual tongue-tied self, so she was shocked when he phoned her. She didn't even tell her mother about him for nearly two months. By then she'd come to realize Barry had enough to say for both of them.

Her mother had been absolutely gleeful!

Her late bloomer had a boyfriend at last.

Shayla sighed, tugged the collar of her shirt into place and wiped the mirror off.

She didn't really want to be thinking about either her mother or Barry right now.

Oh, a little voice chided her, who then?

Him, of course. The cowboy with the wonderful eyes and the voice that sent shivers up and down her spine every time he said anything.

The cowboy, she reminded herself, that had fathered Maria's child and killed some other unnamed woman's plants.

The cowboy who had suggested red candles with dinner.

She could feel the heat in her cheeks, and somewhere else deep inside her, a fire stoking to red hot.

''You're out of your league,'' she told herself sternly.

The phone rang. She was going to let it ring, but it rang and rang and rang. And then it occurred to her it might be Maria!

She abandoned her attempts to do something bewitching with her hair and ran down the hall to the kitchen. She picked up the phone. "Hello."

Dead silence.

"Hello?" she said again.

"Uh—"

A very flustered feminine voice. "Uh, I must have dialed wrong."

"This is Turner MacLeod's residence."

"It is?"

"It is."

Another long pause. "But who are you?"

"Shayla Morrison," she said very unforthcomingly.

"Could you tell Turner Abby called?" The woman sounded like she was going to faint. "Please?"

"Certainly," Shayla said formally and hung up. Why did she delight in stirring up a little havoc in the life of a man she barely knew?

Retribution for Maria and Nicky. Not to mention the dead plants.

Or maybe she sensed in him his deep need to be in control, and took mischievous delight in thwarting that.

It occurred to her she'd been battling controlling people in underground ways for years. And it occurred to her, even by coming here, she was saying, "No more." She was taking to the battlefield above ground now.

Poor Turner.

She forced herself to get some blank music sheets out of her suitcase and went into his living room.

Like the rest of the house it was plain as a monk's chamber. It contained a relatively new sofa in soft shades of beige that reminded her of cold porridge. A matching chair, a coffee table and a TV, all equally lacking in character, finished the ensemble.

A saddle blanket thrown carelessly on the floor beside the chair provided the only splash of color, a beautiful blending of turquoise and reds.

On closer inspection there was a sewing kit beside it, and she found the small rip he was going to repair.

On impulse she held the blanket up to the wall over the sofa, liked it, and tacked it up with a few pins from the sewing kit.

Poor Turner, she thought again. Gleefully.

"Think Halloween show not interior design," she told herself firmly, sitting down on the couch. It was very comfortable. She should have known he would choose it for comfort and not looks.

"Halloween," she told herself again, "not Turner MacLeod."

She scribbled on the paper, mumbling and humming furiously to herself, "Witch and goblin and monster night...watch out Poppy or you'll get a fright. Oh, how I hope the bats don't bite—"

She threw her pencil at the wall and scrunched up the piece of paper.

She went and looked out the window. He had a front yard of sorts, a patch of dry grass, a modest brick fire pit, one poor shrub bent by the ravages of the wind. Beyond that, the landscape was beautiful in the dying light—softened, full of mystery and promise. The land rolled away from her, immense, untamed. The only thing made by man was the ribbon of road that twisted through that ocean of swaying grass. Other than that there was not even a fence post.

She stood there for a long, long time, not able to tear herself away, wishing she was a painter instead of a writer of humble songs, that she could capture the scene before her—immense indigo sky meeting endless golden land—forever in canvas and paint.

"Halloween," she reminded herself sternly.

She retrieved her pencil and went and sat back down on the couch. Where was he? At the barn? The corrals? Which window would she be able to see him from?

"Halloween," she reminded herself. She looked at the fresh piece of paper. "Vampire, vampire, eyes of blue, making up a witches stew—"

Funny the vampire should have blue eyes, she thought. Funny he should be making stew, when that was what the cupboards here were full of.

"I vant to bite your neck," she mumbled to herself, then blushed, picturing the strong column of his neck.

Sometimes in high school, other kids, never her, sported fascinating little purplish marks on their necks called hickeys.

She wondered precisely how one went about making one of those.

"Shayla," she told herself firmly, "you are a writer of songs, not a creator of passionate marks." She forced herself to sing, "What am I going to do, about this vampire with eyes of blue?"

She crumpled up this sheet of paper, too, and threw it on the coffee table. Forget vampires, she told herself. Vampires are not going to work.

The coffee table was covered with magazines about horses. *Horse and Rider. Horse Illustrated. Western Horseman.* They all looked wildly interesting.

Because he was interested in horses?

She deplored women who developed a sudden and rabid interest in the same things that interested a man they were keen on.

"Love at first sight," she wrote on her fresh piece of paper. "Montana skies, love at first sight, midnight eyes."

She stared at it, absolutely appalled with herself. She crumpled up that piece of paper and then changed her mind and tore it into tiny pieces. "What does that have to do with Halloween?" she remonstrated herself.

She picked up her first piece of paper and smoothed the wrinkles out of it. Really, this wasn't so bad. The back door squeaked open.

He was home.

And she felt something flutter in her heart like a million doves taking off.

Something very, very bad was happening to sensible Shayla.

"Hi," she said, getting to her feet and going through the kitchen to the back door.

He was pulling his boots off.

He straightened. Something darkened in his eyes. He was sweat-stained and dirty and about as gorgeous as a man could get.

"Hi," he said back.

"I made you some pizza for supper. I'll just put it in the oven if you want to go get cleaned up."

"Pizza?" he repeated. "You made *me* pizza?"

She smiled at the look of boyish wonder on his face. Like nobody had ever made him dinner before.

Ha-ha, don't get taken in by it, Shayla. She'd be

willing to bet he'd had a lot of mighty fine dinners laid his feet—crab and escargot, lobster and coq au vin.

This was a very dangerous game she was playing, she realized. Just like a little wife waiting at the door for her man to come home.

Why would she, who had always prided herself on her independence, find any enjoyment in that particular role? She who rejected the whole idea of a man as essential to a rich and satisfying life—especially the more her mother pushed it.

"I'll hit the shower," he said.

If she were his wife she would hit the shower with him.

The very thought made her turn crimson.

A few minutes later she heard the water pounding down, and the sound was so intimate it made her throat go dry.

She was in here putting the final touches on the pizza—and the red candles on the table—and he was in there without a stitch on.

She was feeling things she had simply never felt. Wild things. Animal things.

Her mother would tell her to cut and run. Her mother had often told her, "The more handsome the man, the more you can't trust him."

Shayla put the pizza on the table. She lit the candles and turned off the lights just as he came in, freshly shaved, his hair wet and curling, a crisp new shirt tucked into pressed jeans.

Their eyes met.

He came slowly across the room. He only glanced at the pizza.

He's going to kiss me, she thought with wild anticipation.

"It sure smells good in here," he said with that slow, soft drawl that made her heart turn over like an Indy car engine.

"Thank you," she said huskily. He was standing very close to her now, looking down at her in the soft, golden light.

He leaned closer.

Remember Maria, she thought desperately. Remember dead flowers.

He brushed his hand across her face and held it up for her to see.

"Flour," she said weakly. The texture of his hands remained in her mind, the skin work- and weather-roughened, the calluses hard, the sensation heart stopping.

"Looks like you were slapping it on like Bo-Bo the clown."

And she'd thought he was going to kiss her? And that unfortunate reference to a clown! She was going to have to call Barry...the clown. And her mother.

Her eyes wandered to the cowboy's lips. She would have rather he kissed her.

Oh, my God, she thought, I've lost my mind. Was her life so dissatisfying to her she was now indulging in fantasies while she was awake? Still, at the very thought of his lips touching hers, her limbs felt like they had turned to water. Her heart felt like it would pound out of her chest. Her face felt crimson underneath the flattering white powder.

Shayla, she reprimanded herself, remember real life. Halloween songs. Barry. Mother. But if she remembered anything at all, it was an age-old remembrance, of man and woman, of what they were meant to be to one another.

He pulled back from her, still too close, scanning her eyes, reading her face.

Too fast, she told herself. If you go too fast, girl, you are going to be sorry.

No speed limits in Montana, another little voice inside her head reminded her.

The strength radiated from him. His scent filled her nostrils, strong and clean and good. One-hundred-percent man.

''Me hungry. Now.''

Turner turned swiftly, and she started and realized she must have been leaning toward him because she lost her balance and stumbled forward an awkward little half step. He caught her elbow and gave her a look that burned with amusement.

Nicky was standing in the doorway, glowering at them.

The little boy looked much better, though he was eyeing them with a look she could only have called suspicious.

A reminder that she, Shayla the Sensible, had just completely lost her senses! And it had felt incredible!

''Well then, let's eat,'' she said brightly. She rubbed a sleeve quickly over her face.

''Too dark,'' Nicky grumbled, taking one of the two chairs at the table.

She flipped on the light. Turner gave her another look, measuring this time, obviously making some judgment, because she allowed herself to be bossed around by a three-year-old.

"It's not that big a deal whether the light is on or off," she said defensively.

"I didn't say anything," he said. But he had. Those piercing blue eyes had spoken volumes. "Nicky, I'll get another chair. You go get a pillow to sit on."

Nicky looked at him mutinously, settled himself more firmly, and then picked up his fork and looked at the pizza.

Turner folded his arms across his chest.

The contest of wills lasted a full minute before Nicky shot Turner a disgruntled look, then got up.

"Really, I can get one," Shayla said. "He's only three."

"He's big enough to haul a pillow! And big enough to learn some manners."

The words sounded hard, but there was no mistaking the rough affection in Turner's eyes as he watched the boy disappear down the hall. He turned back to her, and the affection still warmed his eyes.

"Nobody ever cooked me pizza before. It looks really good." He went into the living room and came back with a straight-backed chair.

"Well, let's eat before it gets cold," she said, her voice too bright again.

She cut the pizza, but when she moved to go find Nicky, a firm hand on her arm stayed her. Turner shook his head. "Let him do it."

Nicky arrived, eventually, and looking quite pleased with himself. She noted the pillow he had found did not appear to be the one that had been on his bed.

"My pillow," Turner said with a grin.

Nicky carefully placed the pillow on the empty

chair, climbed up on it and wriggled his bottom on it with great satisfaction.

"Think he's trying to tell me something?" Turner asked.

"Me pizza, *now*."

"Pizza, please," Turner corrected him quietly.

Nicky lowered his dark brow in his famous scowl. One of Turner's own dark brows shot up.

"Please," Nicky gave in with ill grace.

She dished out the pizza, and self-consciously bit in, wishing suddenly she'd made something that was more dignified to eat.

"This is great," Turner said with such genuine enthusiasm that she decided to make pizza for every meal.

If she ever made another meal. Which she wasn't going to. She was making that promise to herself right now.

He could cook next time. Equal rights and all that stuff. If there was a next time. Maria could call at any minute.

The thought should thrill her. Her gaze fastened on his lips and his teeth. She was willing to bet they tasted far better than the pizza, which was passably good considering the lack of selection for ingredients.

These thoughts shocked her. She suddenly feared he might read her mind, see this wantonness in there.

Conversation, she ordered herself. "You certainly like apples."

"I do?"

"And carrots."

"Oh, you mean in the fridge."

"The only fresh things in the house."

He looked sheepish. "I buy them for the horses."

"Me six," Nicky announced, sending Turner a sidelong glance.

"Small for your age?" Turner asked dryly.

"Pop, *now*," Nicky ordered Shayla.

"Does he get away with this?" Turner asked, astounded.

"He's only three."

"I thought he was six," Turner said. "Nicky, if you want something to drink, you have to ask for it differently."

"Pop, *now*, Poppy." Nicky giggled. "Pop, Poppy, pop."

"Night-night, Nicky, night-night," Turner returned in a low warning growl.

"Please pop," Nicky capitulated.

"Milk," Turner said.

"You don't have any," she pointed out.

He got up and got a Tetra pack of milk from a cupboard she had missed.

Nicky got milk. He looked at it sulkily, blew bubbles in it, made a few vulgar noises.

"Is he like this all the time?" Turner asked Shayla.

She felt a sudden stab of anger. How dare he sit in judgement of the small boy that he had not helped raise?

"He needs a man in his life. I can't stand it when you guys do this. Abandon a child like there's no more to being a father than planting a seed, then complaining bitterly when you see how mothers raise their kids alone."

He stared at her. Something glittered in his eyes.

To her it seemed like pain and regret, but his words belied that.

"You think he's mine."

She studied Turner and Nicky. Except for the eye color, they could have been twins sitting there scowling darkly at her.

"Isn't he?" she demanded softly.

"I don't think we should be having this conversation in front of him."

Childishly she wanted to tell him he had started it.

The phone rang. Glaring at her, he got up from his chair and crossed to the counter.

"I forgot to tell you Abby called," she said innocently, taking a bite of her pizza.

He threw her a nasty look. How could she stand to make pizza for him if she harbored in her heart the hard little thought this was his boy sitting here? That he'd abandoned him?

And now she blithely informed him Abby had called as if her answering the phone in his house wouldn't have all kinds of repercussions.

Abby knew he had company. And if he knew his sister she wasn't going to rest until she knew who it was.

He would let it ring, but Abby had an aggravating habit of thinking he was at the barn and that the minute he heard the phone ring he started dashing for the house.

She always let it ring at least sixty times before she hung up.

He hadn't gotten around to telling her he couldn't hear his phone ringing from the barn, and he wouldn't have made a run for it even if he could.

Abby had suggested a phone in the barn.

Didn't she know there were sacred places?

At least that most horrible of inventions, the answering machine, was not even a possibility out here with their shared phone lines.

"Hello," he said reluctantly. "Abby. I thought it might be you.... Nobody's more surprised than me.... That's a long story.... You have time? Well, I'm kind of in the middle of something.... What! geez...we're on a party line, you'll give May Swanson a heart attack—" he heard the distinctive click of May hanging up guiltily "—dinner. I'm in the middle of dinner."

The kid started yelling about more milk.

"Please," he reminded him sternly, putting his hand over the receiver. "Yeah, you heard a kid...a little boy.... That's right. I have a whole secret life I never told you about. So secret in fact, I never knew about it myself."

This earned him a baleful glance from the pizza chef. "The boy is Maria Gerrardi's son," he said. "It appears you have a nephew."

His sister squealed so loud he had to hold the phone away from his ear. But Shayla's eyes appeared to grow larger and darker as the blood drained from her face.

Oh, so maybe Shayla hadn't really believed the worst of him before. He guessed that she did now.

Abby, of course, knew all about Maria and Nick. Shayla had had no idea.

Well, he wasn't about to sit down and give her a crash course in the MacLeod family history.

It was probably better that she believed what she

believed. Why would he want to kiss a woman who thought so badly of him without a shred of evidence?

His eyes found her lips. Why indeed?

But if she had any sense, she'd probably keep her distance from him now. And she looked like the sensible type.

The funny thing was that when he'd brushed that dusting of flour from her face, and she'd leaned toward him, she hadn't seemed like the sensible type. Not even a little bit.

"What about Nick?" he asked Abby. "Not me... Not a word.... No, Abby, please don't come over. He's your nephew and you have a right? Okay, if you must. Bring a couple of green peppers with you." He said this in a low tone he hoped Shayla hadn't heard. He cast her a glance. From the mutinous look on her face he might as well cancel the green peppers. She wasn't cooking him pizza again anytime in the near future.

"No, that wasn't Maria who answered the phone. It's a long story.... I know *you* have time. I don't!"

After a few more tortured minutes trying to convince his sister to at least wait until morning to make the acquaintance of the nephew she sounded absolutely thrilled about, he slammed down the phone.

"Who's Nick?" Shayla asked quietly.

"*Me* Nicky."

"My brother," he said coldly.

"Is Nicky his or yours?"

"You figure it out," he said coldly.

"That's not fair."

Like life was fair.

"Nicky Shayla's and Mommy's," the little boy informed him. "Nicky not yours. Nicky like Shayla. Nicky like Mommy. Nicky like Ralph. Nicky like horses. Nicky like pizza. Nicky don't like you." And then he took a large and unconcerned bite of his pizza.

If life was fair, this would not be happening to him—two people who seemed to dislike him very much dropping in from nowhere to complicate his uncomplicated life.

Why enlighten her? Abby would look after that in about three seconds tomorrow.

He only hoped he could find some urgent business that needed tending in Billings.

For tonight a little chilled distance between him and that hazel-eyed vixen was probably best. It was the only answer really to what had leaped up between them only a short while ago.

He had been stunned by that. That sudden feeling, when he saw her standing across the room, of *knowing* her, of having always known her.

It had seemed like the most natural thing in the world to cross the room, look down at her, brush the flour from her face.

And think renegade thoughts about kissing her.

Thoughts as unstoppable as the storm.

The storm that was coming.

Geez, he could smell it. In the air, on the wind.

He met her eyes.

He could see it, brewing right there.

Chapter Four

The sofa bed hurt his back. She'd said absolutely not when he'd offered her his bed, but he'd won out. If he could call this winning...trying to sleep in his living room on a bed that felt like it was waiting to spring shut the moment his eyes closed.

Something was different about the living room. He couldn't quite figure out what. It seemed cozier somehow.

Could a woman do that with her mere presence?

He tossed and turned and got up at least a dozen times for water, and the more tired he became, the more his mind wandered to her lips. And eyes. The honey color of her hair. And especially that voice. It was with his mind mulling over her voice that he finally slept.

And woke to find two large dark eyes staring into his. The boy's face was only about a half inch from his, and the short distance made Nicky look like a little owl.

"Uh, good morning, Nicky." He closed his eyes again. He really hadn't felt this awful since those long-ago days when the rodeo had meant too many bruises, too many drinks and too many uncomfortable nights in motel beds that felt exactly like this one.

He wished he'd had the foresight to try out this stupid bed while it was still at the furniture store.

"Nicky like horses," Nicky announced.

He opened one eye a crack. Nicky was still close enough to make him go cross-eyed.

He sat up and groaned. Just past dawn. His back was killing him. His head felt fuzzy from lack of sleep.

"Horses," Nicky said. "Please, horses."

"You want to help me feed them?"

A solemn nod.

"You feeling better?"

Another solemn nod.

"Are my boots safe today?"

The glimmer of a smile so like his brother's was at that age made Turner feel a funny choking sensation in his throat.

"Okay. Go get dressed. Meet me back here in five minutes."

Nicky was back in two, just as Turner did up the snap on his own jeans. Turner folded up the bed and replaced the cushions. He regarded the room thoughtfully.

It was still bugging him. Something was different, but he couldn't put his finger on it.

"Ralph come?" Nicky asked, holding up the dinosaur.

"As long as he doesn't eat my horses."

Nicky laughed, a little rumbling sound deep down in his belly.

When they went out the door, Turner was astounded to find a chubby hand reach up for his.

As soon as he took it, the truth slammed into him. He had to find his brother. He had to mend fences.

Time marched on. Little boys became big boys and then men. You could never have back the moments you had missed or thrown away.

Stupid to have been stubborn as long as he had. Stupid to have waited for Nick to make the first move, when it had been Turner who had done wrong.

He could see that so clearly now. Who was he to have said what should be? If he'd had his way, this little boy wouldn't even be on the earth right now, and he could feel the loss in that.

This little guy was meant to be here.

And Turner MacLeod was not meant to have any say in these things.

The things that he'd thought were his to control, he'd made a mess of.

Nicky dropped his beloved dinosaur facedown in the dust as soon as he saw the horses.

Turner had four of them in for training right now, not counting the hell-horse and his personal riding horses over in the pasture. They were gathered at the fence waiting for breakfast.

Nicky scrambled up the fence with such velocity he nearly plunged over the other side.

Turner plucked him off the fence and introduced him to each one. He gave the horses quick one-syllable names that they would respond to easily, and he'd long since given up on using his imagination.

The naming process took him about one second per horse. He'd called these ones Stock, Doc, Rock, and Shoe.

Nicky rechristened each horse tenderly. "Thunderboy," he proclaimed Stock. Doc became Zippity, Rock became Chance, and Shoe he called Marmalade.

After naming them, Nicky whispered a little secret in each of their ears, touching them with stubby fingers that were exquisitely gentle. Turner enjoyed the moment more than he ever could have guessed he would.

He hay- and grain-fed the four horses, and Nicky proudly carried an alfalfa flake out to drop through the fence to each horse. Then Turner gave him the grain buckets and watched as he climbed the fence and distributed some into each box.

"Good job, little man."

Nicky beamed, his sturdy little chest swelling with pride.

"One left," Turner told him handing him the refilled oat bucket. "Behind the barn there."

He grabbed a flake of alfalfa hay, and couldn't keep from smiling at how Nicky was strutting with the importance of his job.

They went around the barn to the small pen behind it.

Nicky gasped, and set down the bucket and ran right toward the fence. "Pretty!" he crowed.

Turner juggled his handful of hay and caught up Nicky with his other arm.

"She's not trained yet, Nicky. She's mean. She might bite you."

Nicky didn't take his eyes off her. "Nicky pet *now*."

"No," Turner said. "Later you might be able to pet her."

Later? Was there going to be a later for him and this little boy?

Or for him and this horse? She was going to take everything he had and then some. He slid a look at his little visitor and thought of his not-so-little visitor at the house. Maybe this horse was one wild female he'd leave alone for a while.

Not to suggest, of course, that he was going to be chasing the other one around the house.

Firmly he made himself focus on the horse. Pretty didn't say half of it, really. She was a leopard-spotted Appaloosa, her body white, covered from the tip of her nose to her hind quarters with black dots the size of fifty-cent pieces to the size of tennis balls.

He was usually a quarter horse man but from the minute he'd seen her he'd found her irresistible.

Which was stupid. Too many of the wrong things had been done to her already. She distrusted people with everything she had.

He didn't know if that could be fixed.

But this morning, more than ever, he wanted to believe that mistakes could be fixed. That this horse could be given a second chance, and that people could, too.

"Nicky pet *now*."

Turner curbed the impatience he felt at that demanding *now*. "Somebody hurt her, Nicky. She's angry. She might hurt you. You have to stay away from her."

"Like her," Nicky said.

"Yeah," Turner said. "Me, too."

"Nicky hungry *now*."

The *now* was not snapped out like an order.

They put the hay and grain in the Appaloosa's pen. She stood squashed as far back against the fence as she could.

"Don't be scared," Nicky called to her. "Nicky like you." His chubby little hand found Turner's again. "Nicky like you, too," he decided.

Turner couldn't trust himself to speak. Instead he squeezed the little hand tight, and they walked back up to the house together.

They were just crossing the yard when his sister's motor home pulled in.

His niece, Danielle, just turned six, tumbled out and threw herself at him. He was never quite sure what he did to deserve the vigor of her greetings, but he loved them nonetheless. He obligingly whirled her in circles until she squealed, and then he put her down and ruffled her long blond hair.

Abby, heavily pregnant, was getting down from the motor home. He went and helped her.

"You look beautiful," he told her with a grin. She did. Her gorgeous blond hair hung in a thick braid over her shoulder. But it was her eyes, dark like Nick's—and his son's—that made her look astounding. They glowed with a soft and peaceful light.

"Oh, sure. Me and the refrigerator are about the same size."

But he could tell she was pleased he had said it. And he meant it, too. Abby was radiant with good health and happiness.

At least he'd done something right.

Her eyes found Nicky, who Turner realized had taken up refuge behind his leg.

"Oh!" she said, and tears formed in her eyes. "He's so like Nick!" She shoved a bag of groceries into Turner's hands.

"Hi, there," she said softly. "What's your name?"

"Nicky," he said cautiously, peeping out at her.

"Nicky, I'm your Aunt Abby, and this is your cousin Danielle."

Nicky nodded uncertainly.

"I've got toys in the motor home," Danielle told him. "Do you want to see?"

His nod was vigorous this time. He came out from behind the leg, a little explosion of energy.

Abby laughed. "I brought some bacon and eggs. I didn't know if you had any."

"Ah, you know me. Cheerios in the morning." He glanced in the bag. "Is this blueberry pie?"

They went up the steps to his house together. They heard a shout of laughter from the motor home before the door swung shut behind them.

"We have to tell Nick," Abby said.

"I know."

"I think it's wonderful," she said softly.

"You know what, little sister? I do, too," he admitted, and kissed her on the cheek.

"Oh, you charmer, you. It's been some time since anyone called me little!"

Shayla awoke to silence as complete as any she had ever heard. The faint cry of a far-off hawk, and the wind in the rafters, but nothing else. No cars or airplanes or ambulances.

It was, she mused sleepily, a good place to create music.

She opened her eyes and liked what she saw. Despite the relative plainness of it, she liked his room. It smelled of leather and laundry soap. The bed was a big antique four-poster that his relatives had probably brought here on a covered wagon a hundred years ago.

The top of his bureau was littered with silver belt buckles that she'd discovered had rodeo names and events on them. A saddle, heavy with silver and engraved down the stirrup with the words "Champion 1990," stood on a stand by the window. Chinks and chaps hung off a row of hooks on the back of his door. A selection of ball caps and cowboy hats hung from another row of hooks beside the door.

One wall was covered with framed photographs of horses, many of them being presented with ribbons. Written in a careful hand at the bottom of each picture were names like Blackie, Partner, Brandy and Joe.

There wasn't a picture of a human being in the whole room, she'd noted last night with wry humor.

She stretched, feeling oddly contented. She got up and padded over to the window, then threw it open to the crisp early-autumn air.

The air was so pure it was like drinking cold clear water from a mountain stream.

Just as she was beginning to wonder why Nicky, a notoriously early riser, wasn't up and making a great deal of noise, she saw them.

Nicky and Turner coming up the worn path from

the barn toward the house, little clouds of dust kicking up at their feet, the morning sun framing them in gold.

They were holding hands, and Turner had his head cocked slightly, listening.

Even from here she could hear Nicky's excited jabber, though not the precise words.

She felt the sudden prick of tears at the sight they made. There was strength in the scene, but tenderness and trust, too. On Nicky's face, as they came closer, she could see a look of...contentment, she supposed. She was not sure she had seen that particular expression on his face before.

And though the brim of Turner's hat shaded his face from her, she sensed some ease in him, too, in the wonderful relaxed way he was walking, in the easy way he held that small hand in his large one.

The motor home pulled up and she watched again as a pixieish little girl tumbled out and threw herself at Turner with a complete lack of reserve. Watched him pick her up and whirl her around, and felt something stir deep in her heart, though she knew not what.

She turned quickly from the window, shuffled hurriedly through the contents of the suitcase she'd packed to last her three days at the most.

Out of her limited choices she pulled on purple leggings and a too-large University of Oregon sweatshirt, brushed her hair until it shone, dabbed a hint of lipstick on her mouth and then on her cheeks, since she had forgotten her blush.

She heard them coming to the door and went to meet them.

"Shayla, this is my sister, Abby."

"Hi," Shayla said awkwardly.

"Shayla," Abby said taking her hand in a strong grip, and looking with directness into her eyes. "Thank you so much for bringing my nephew. I'm glad you're here."

The welcome was so full of warmth that Shayla knew everything was going to be all right.

Abby had Turner set down the brown paper sack full of supplies on the counter and began emptying ingredients from it. "Turner, did you notice how Shayla looks like Aunt Marg?"

"Uh, no I didn't."

Abby laughed. "Not thinking Aunt Marg thoughts toward Shayla, are you?"

Shayla's eyes widened and she glanced at him. He was turning a touch red under the sun-weathered gold of his skin.

"So what are we going to do about this?" Abby was taking out bacon and arranging it in neat rows in the pan. "Make some coffee, Turner. What are we going to do?"

"I'll make a few calls today, see if I can track down Maria. And Nick."

Abby turned to him with a satisfied smile at that. "Oh, he'll be so thrilled to know he's a daddy."

Shayla shot Turner a black look. He'd let her believe he was the father! He seemed to be very busy with that coffee.

But, she asked herself, why had she been so ready to believe the worst of him?

Mother. Men according to mother.

The more attractive a man, the more you can't trust him. Or yourself.

"Now," Abby said to Shayla, "you come here and

watch the bacon. I'll start the toast. Where do you fit into all this?''

So Shayla fried bacon and tried to ignore Turner and told his sister all about what had happened.

''She must be planning on coming here,'' Abby said. ''Are you going to stay until she gets here?''

''Well, I really can't stay indefinitely. A day or two at the most. And now that you're here, Nicky will be all right. There's probably really no reason for me to stay at all.''

Did Abby send a slightly sly look between her and Turner?

''Oh,'' Abby said blithely. ''Don't count on me. I'm not due for a month, but I just have a feeling...'' She patted her bulging stomach with satisfaction.

''What kind of feeling?'' Turner asked with such trepidation that both women laughed.

''Women stuff,'' Abby said.

Her announcement made Shayla feel oddly happy. When the motor home had arrived and when Abby had marched in, obviously a very capable woman in any circumstances, she had thought there was no longer any reason for her to stay.

She wanted to stay.

It was that simple.

And that complicated.

Just like the man over there measuring coffee into the coffeemaker with military precision.

''Aren't you scared being so far from a hospital?''

Abby shook her head. ''I've been around this country all my life. There's not much about nature that scares me. Not even twins.''

''Twins?'' Shayla gasped.

"Twins," Turner confirmed bleakly, sending a worried look in the direction of his sister's gigantic tummy.

Abby gave her brother a look of exasperated affection and then said to Shayla, "You're just staying until tomorrow, you say?"

Again that feeling of wanting to stay. To embrace the adventure. To see this thing right through to the ending.

She heard the children shriek with laughter outside.

A happy ending. Who could resist a happy ending?

Why not? She could do her job from here. The more she thought of her mother and Barry, the more she didn't want to go back. She was resisting even making the simple phone call she knew had to be made before her mom and Barry called out the state troopers.

Her mother had even insisted on Shayla leaving her a map. "So they'll know where to look if you go missing, dear."

Why not stay? Because she had not really been invited. She was imposing on this man.

"I should go. Tomorrow." She heard the wishy-washiness in her own voice. Not a good strong statement—*I am leaving tomorrow at 9:00 a.m. sharp*—at all.

Turner turned from the coffeemaker and gave her a look that a woman could read far too much into. Like maybe he wanted her to stay, too. Despite himself.

"Don't be so anxious to go," Abby told her. "This is beautiful country. You should really see it from horseback while you're here."

"Oh," Shayla said with more wistfulness than she intended. "I haven't been on a horse in years."

"Well then, it's settled. Today, we'll see what we can do about tracking down Nick and Maria, and tomorrow Turner can take you for a ride. I'll look after the kids. All right, Turner?"

"Sure," he said noncommittally.

"You probably have people you want to let know where you are."

If it was a statement, it was a probing one.

"My mother," Shayla said, and felt just the tiniest bit guilty for not even mentioning Barry. Why was so much of her relationship with him overlaid with a hint of guilt? "I'll call after breakfast."

Abby called the kids, and they all sat down to a wonderful breakfast.

"Nicky like bacon," Nicky announced grabbing a mittful right off the plate.

"Don't be a piggy," Danielle told him prissily.

Nicky oinked at her.

She oinked back.

He crossed his eyes, pushed up his nose with his finger, making a horrible snout. He wuffled convincingly.

She did the same.

Turner looked at his sister, who passed him the salt with a pleasant smile and a loud oink of her own. Shayla cracked up.

"Shayla's turn. Piggy," Nicky ordered.

She clutched her stomach, doubled over from laughing and oinked obligingly. She managed to lift her head and make her best piggy face.

The kids howled. Turner looked at her with disbelief.

"Uncle Turner, your turn," Danielle cackled.

"Turner turn," Nicky agreed loudly.

He looked like he wanted nothing more than to have them all carted off to the nuthouse.

And then he shrugged, and snorted loudly.

Danielle's mouth fell open. So did Abby's. Nicky grinned. Shayla stared.

"What?" he said.

"That was very good," Abby said, raising her coffee mug to him. "I'd about given up hope on you, Turner."

"What? You didn't think I'd ever perfect my pig imitation?"

"No," she said softly. "I didn't think you'd ever learn how to play."

"I play out there with those horses all the time," he said defensively. "It's how I make my living. Playing."

"Some people might call that work."

"Well, they'd be wrong, speaking of which I do have work—I mean playing—to do." He deliberately set his face in firm lines. "I've got to work those colts before I make any phone calls."

"Fine, you go ahead. Shayla and I will visit." Abby nodded toward the archway where she could look into his living room. "By the way, that blanket hanging up over the couch looks right homey."

"What blanket?" he asked blackly.

Shayla studied a piece of bacon, fighting an irresistible urge to give in again to giggles. Oh my, when had she laughed like this? When had her existence become so darned serious? So dull?

He stomped into the living room. Silence. A moment later, the offending blanket tucked possessively under his arm, he went out the door.

Abby and Shayla howled with laughter.

The kids looked at them wide-eyed and then began to laugh, too.

It was such a simple moment and yet so fine.

"He needs a family," Abby said, looking after her brother with affection. "You know my parents died when he was only seventeen. He raised my brother and me. He took it very seriously. He was very strict with Nick and me. But I think being thrust into that role too young kind of soured him on settling down.

"There was a girl up the road he was quite taken with in his twenties, but he'd already had too much responsibility. He didn't want to get married and start having kids, he'd just gotten free of raising two! Plus I think the fact he and Nick are estranged has made him believe he did a rotten job of it, when really that's not true at all. Given his age I think he did quite a remarkable job of it.

"Give me a hand clearing up. I want to hear all about you."

To determine if she was a candidate for settling down with her brother, Shayla thought uneasily. Of course she wasn't. She lived in Portland. She had never given a single thought to moving. She had her job to think of.

Even if she was thinking of settling down, why would she pick a man like him? Okay, he was so handsome it took her breath away. Okay, she could listen to his deep voice forever. Okay, he was intriguing.

But he was so controlling he couldn't even stand a blanket being hung up on his wall.

And really, after surviving a mother like hers, controlling people were out of the question.

Abby was probably telling her his whole life story by now, he thought, checking over his equipment, assembling ropes and blankets, halters and an old saddle. As if anybody would find that the least bit intriguing.

He'd hated when the kids at the table started making faces at each other and laughing hysterically, getting completely out of control.

Then he'd thought, so what? They weren't his kids. He'd deliberately made himself let go of control, thinking Abby or Shayla would step in.

Ha. They got right into the spirit of it. Had fun over breakfast.

"Not exactly a hanging offense," he muttered to himself, slinging the ropes over his shoulder, and bracing the saddle against his hip.

He'd never allowed himself to have much fun with Nick and Abby, once his folks had died. He supposed he'd been scared that if he ever let himself go, they would have lost respect for him, that everything would have fallen apart.

That probably was why he had turned to training horses. It was an enjoyment he could allow himself. Hard work, but deeply satisfying. Fun wasn't too strong a word.

The kids' laughter lingered in his mind, made him grin foolishly. So did Shayla's.

He'd taken that blanket off the wall and then regretted it. Why had it bugged him? It wasn't hurting anything. It had looked nice up there.

Maybe Nick had been right about him. He had to control every little thing, even things that didn't matter.

If he was anything of a man, he'd put that blanket right back up there. He sighed and set it aside to take back to the house with him later.

He found he was feeling oddly eager to be back there, part of that circle of laughter.

He went out into the corral and whistled, high and piercing through his teeth. The horses turned to him, ears pricked, looking alert and willing.

A good bunch, he thought stepping toward them, his focus now shifting entirely to them, everything else fading.

"Okay, Marmalade," he said. "You're up."

Shayla dialed the number with trepidation, hoping she would get the answering machine, but she didn't.

"Shayla," her mother squealed. "Where have you been?"

"Around the world in a canoe. In three days! I'm going to be in the Guinness book."

A little silence met her remark. "I was just concerned about you. Are you being sarcastic?"

"I thought I was being funny."

"Well, you weren't."

Three days ago Shayla would have apologized. But now she'd driven seventy-three miles an hour. It changed everything.

"I'm going to stay for a few days, Ma."

"Where?"

"At Nicky's uncle's place. In Montana."

Her mother was silent. "His *aunt* and uncle's place?"

She realized she could be misleading now if she wanted to be. After all, Nicky did have an aunt and an uncle on the premises at the moment.

But she didn't want to be misleading.

"Just his uncle's."

"His uncle is single?"

Shayla said nothing.

"Is he handsome, Shayla? Is he?"

"Ma, I'll be home in a few days."

"A few days? What am I supposed to tell Barry?"

"Uh, tell him hello. From me."

"Shayla, don't do anything foolish. I knew this was foolish—"

"Ma, I'm on a party line. I can't tie it up."

"Yes, you can! Unless the other party has an emergency you're perfectly entitled to talk to your poor old mother."

"How do you know that? About emergencies?"

"I read it in the phone book."

"You're reading the phone book?"

"That's what old, *lonely* people do."

"Fifty-two is not old." I'm being sucked in, Shayla thought, even though I didn't bite on the "lonely" part, I've opened the door for her to talk about her bursitis.

"I feel old," her mother said. "The bursitis was so bad this morning—"

"Ma, I'm safe. I'm happy—"

"Happy?" her mother said with alarm.

"And I'm staying."

"Staying? But you can't!"

"Ma, I'm twenty-four years old. I guess I can if I want to."

Silence, and then a tiny, hurt "But for how long?"

"A few days."

"Shayla, have you lost your mind?"

"Yes," she said, and hung up.

She waited for the guilt to twist in her stomach, but it didn't. Instead she felt herself smiling.

Free.

If it weren't for those damned Halloween songs she would be one hundred percent free.

"Vampire, vampire," she hummed.

But the tune was a different one. Montana skies. Midnight eyes.

Outside the window she saw Abby clearing the flower box. She went and joined her.

Danielle and Nicky were running around and around the house, riding a broom and a mop named Thunderboy and Marmalade.

The sunshine felt good on her cheeks.

"I don't know why I bother," Abby said, eyeing a dead geranium with disgust before depositing it in the large green garbage bag beside her.

"You planted these flowers?"

"Does *he* look like the type?" Abby asked with a snort.

The answer told Shayla quite a lot. That Turner had been without a woman in his life for a long, long time.

"Not hardly," Shayla said, trying to ignore the funny singing of her heart.

Chapter Five

He worked the horses for about an hour before Shayla showed up, obviously being dragged along by Danielle and Nicky. The four colts weren't used to strangers, and it wrecked their concentration.

His, too.

"Sorry," she called. "They insisted."

"It's okay. It's good for him," he said of the colt who was watching them, wide-eyed and wuffling softly at his audience, not paying the least bit of attention to Turner.

Out of the corner of his eye, he saw Shayla was carrying an armful of grass. He focused on the colt, made him give him back his undivided attention.

"What's his name, Uncle Turner?" Danielle called.

"Rock. Sorry, I mean Chance."

"Oh," Danielle said with approval. "Just like in *Homeward Bound*."

"Nicky name," Nicky crowed so loudly that the colt started and stared at him.

"He's sacking him out," Danielle explained importantly to Shayla. "Aren't you, Uncle Turner?"

"Yeah," he growled. He tried to ignore them. Those tight purple things on Shayla's legs were making him feel as skittish and shy as the colt.

"What does that mean?" Shayla whispered.

"He hits the horse with that blanket until the horse stops hating it and starts liking it."

Not a bad explanation, Turner thought. The colt was already calming. Instead of leaping every time the blanket touched him, he was just starting a bit. Soon, he was just standing quietly.

Turner tossed the blanket over the colt's head, and left it.

His audience laughed, just as Turner had known they would. The colt peeked out from under his makeshift hat cautiously, and he laughed, too.

"Okay, big fella," he said, "enough school for today." Turner took the blanket off and led the colt over to the kids.

"Pet," Nicky yelled.

"Nicky, try not to scare him," Shayla said.

"Actually," Turner said, "the more noise he makes the better. You don't want a horse that spooks at every little sound. A little later in his training, I hook bells up to him, and milk jugs full of rocks. It's all about him learning he can trust me, trust my judgment above his own."

"It's fascinating," she said.

"You know, I've been doing this since I was a kid, and it still fascinates me. I still learn something new every single day. What more can a man ask of life than that?''

Not to be lonely, a renegade voice deep inside himself answered.

''Come on, kids,'' he said gruffly. ''I've got to make some phone calls.'' He let the colt go and joined them on the other side of the fence.

''Want to see pretty horse,'' Nicky said.

''Me, too,'' Danielle said. ''Mommy says she's crazy.''

Shayla looked at him quizzically.

''I got me a bit of a renegade horse,'' he admitted. ''Come have a look, then.''

Shayla reacted like everyone reacted. ''She's beautiful,'' she breathed. ''I've never seen a horse like that.''

''Appaloosa,'' he said. ''A leopard-spot.'' For some reason, it flashed through his mind how fine Shayla would look riding this horse. A ridiculous thought.

''What's wrong with her? Why does your sister think she's crazy?''

''She's wild. And mean. She kicks, bites and strikes.''

''Then you're the crazy one. Because you adore her,'' Shayla said, turning to him with a smile, but in that smile he saw understanding.

''Would you try something for me?'' he asked on impulse.

''What's that?''

''Could you try singing to her? I read somewhere it has a calming effect on them. I've never tried it though. I'm not much of a singer.''

For a moment it looked like she might refuse, but then she turned and walked over to the fence and regarded the wildly colorful horse thoughtfully. Then she sang:

"Wild lady,
Are you really crazy,
Or do you have some hurt inside,
Waiting, waiting, waiting,
Wild lady,
Love will abide."

Her voice was soft and soothing, the melody haunting. The words sent tingles up and down his spine.

And so did the effect it had on the horse.

The hell-horse stopped pawing, her ears came forward.

Shayla stopped.

"Sing it again," he requested softly.

She sang it again and then again. The horse sighed, as if some burden was being lifted off her shoulders, took a cautious step or two toward them, then stopped. Her head dropped slightly and her weight came off her back left foot.

One more verse, and the horse would go to sleep.

"That's incredible," he said softly.

"But does it help?"

"I don't know," he said. "Maybe I can figure out a way to make it help."

"You sing real good," Danielle told her.

"Thanks," she said almost shyly.

How could she have a voice like that and be shy about it?

"Sing 'Poppy Pepperseed,'" Nicky demanded as they all turned away from the horse.

"Oh, I don't think so—"

"Please," Danielle implored.

Please, Turner thought. Her voice had the same bloody effect on him that it had on the horse. It tamed something wild inside him, made him feel easy and relaxed and like the world was good.

It made him yearn after some things. Things he had not had for years. Like coming home to the smell of cookies and his mother's smile, his father's hand on his shoulder after they'd worked a young horse together.

He shook his head. A world gone in the blink of an eye.

Son, they're dead. The plane went down. No one lived.

Afraid to want things too much after that. Afraid to be soft. Afraid of losing control. Okay. Afraid of loving.

"Please," Danielle said again. "Sing."

Shayla gave in:

"Poppy Pepperseed's comin' for tea,
Poppy Pepperseed loves me.
We're going to have such a good time,
Laughing and singing and making things rhyme."

The haunting quality was gone from her voice. This little song was fast and rollicking.

"Poppy Pepperseed is my best friend,
And I'm going to love her until childhood's end."

And beyond, he thought, and then gave himself a shake. She was working some kind of strange magic on him, Poppy Pepperseed was.

Satisfied with the song, the kids took off at a dead run up the path in front of them. Nicky shouted with laughter, trying to get his stubby legs to go as fast as those of his colt-legged cousin.

"I've never seen Nicky quite so...happy," she said thoughtfully. "Not that he was unhappy, but—"

"Kids need to be around other kids, I think."

"It's this country, too. Big. Wild. Loud noises and running are okay here. Nicky lives in an apartment in Portland."

Turner didn't want to think of Nicky living in an apartment. He was a boy so full of energy he practically vibrated with it. He was a boy made to chase through long grass, to discover kittens in the hayloft, to fall in the water trough and off fat ponies.

Had he stolen from that boy the childhood he was meant to have? Would Nicky have grown up here with his mom and dad, if Turner hadn't interfered?

Or would the romance between Maria and his brother have died a natural death given time?

He sighed.

"Hey, you guys," he called after the departing children. "You stay away from those horses unless I'm with you.

"Let's go see about finding Maria," he said to Shayla. But he was aware in his mind of a reluctance to find her too quickly. Because when he found Maria, Shayla would go.

There was a note on the table saying Abby had gone to the motor home for a nap. He forced himself to find his directory and pick up the phone.

He needn't have worried. Everybody he talked to, and that seemed to be half the county, couldn't remember the last time people had lived in that Gerrardi shack. Joel at the junction service station thought Milly at the post office might know where they had gone, but she didn't.

After nearly half an hour of dead ends, he gave up on Maria and started on his brother. He called the park office where that TV show had said his brother was employed.

The whole time he was talking, he covertly watched as Shayla arranged some stems of grass in an old chipped enamel milk jug—cutting it to different lengths, going outside and coming back in with a new stalk, one that he wouldn't have given a second thought to as he trampled it under his boot. It was starting to look like some sort of work of art on his kitchen table.

Finally she finished. She walked around it several times, studying it from different angles and then gave a small nod of satisfaction. A simple thing. An old dented milk container full of weeds and grass. The kitchen looked like a different room because of it.

With the smell of cookies baking it would almost feel like…damn. Like a home.

The phone glued to his ear, pretending not to be the least bit interested in her, he charted her next move.

"What do women do out here," Celia had asked him sarcastically, "take up knitting?"

Celia hadn't been a knitter.

Shayla wandered into the living room, tucked those delectable purple-clad legs under her, pulled a pencil from behind her ear and began to hum and jot.

Something about Poppy and a vampire.

He closed his eyes. Only yesterday everything had been so simple, had seemed like it would never change.

"Nick MacLeod," he said to yet another person on the phone. "A family emergency. I know he's up on a mountain. I saw him on TV. The closest ranger station? Yeah, great." He jotted down the number.

"Black cats and witches' cackles,
Poppy, doesn't it just raise your hackles..."

The phone at the closest ranger station rang and rang and rang. He was quite content to listen to it with one ear, and her with the other. Still, he was about to hang up when a man answered.

"End of the Road."

Great. His brother had ended up at a place called End of the Road. As if Turner wasn't feeling guilty enough!

"I'm looking for Nick MacLeod." He reminded himself he was dealing with the government. He'd have to ask in triplicate.

"Geez. You and half the rest of the western world."

"Pardon?"

"He doesn't want to write a book. He doesn't want to be in movies. He doesn't want to meet your sister."

"Thank you. He's already met my sister. Who happens to be his sister."

"Oh, gosh, I'm sorry. Who are you?"

"His brother, Turner."

The man apologized again. "The guy hasn't had a call in three years. Not even a letter as far as I know, and then that segment on TV, and the whole world is trying to find him. Sorry I was rude, but I'm starting to feel like his bloody agent. I didn't come here to the back of beyond because I like answering telephones. Anyway, you missed Nick. He hates the attention. He's taken a couple of weeks' leave."

"Have you got a number where I can reach him?"

"I don't."

Something in the other man's tone of voice told Turner something. Nick wasn't alone when he left his mountain retreat.

"Who's he with? That blond woman who interviewed him?"

"No. Not that she didn't try. Some long-lost friend saw that thing on TV and hiked up there to his cabin. They came down together. He didn't look too unhappy about that part, actually."

"A girlfriend?"

"Mary. Marie. Something like that."

"If you hear from him, tell him to call his brother. It's urgent."

"Somebody die?"

Turner heard Nicky coming in the back door, shrieking.

"Nicky have lunch *now*."

"No," he said. "But somebody's about to." He hung up the phone and leveled a look at his nephew.

"Don't yell like that in the house," he said. "Especially when someone's on the phone."

"'Kay," Nicky agreed amiably. "Nicky like you *now*."

Yup. Someone was about to bite it. Or something. Maybe that stone-cold excuse he'd had for a heart.

He went into the living room. She was sitting with her legs tucked under her, her hair falling in a curtain over her face, tongue caught between pearly teeth.

The place above her head where the saddle blanket had hung looked empty and cold.

Poppy had turned into a pumpkin seed.

"It sounds like they're together," he said. "Maria and Nick."

Something lit behind her eyes, making them dance with green and gold.

A believer, he thought, in romance, in happy endings, in fairy tales.

He was a man who'd spent just a little too much time with manure on his boots to put too much stock in stuff that wasn't nitty-gritty real.

"They're together?" she breathed.

He nodded. "But I don't know where."

"Oh." She said this as if it didn't matter where they were.

"Is Abby still napping?" he asked, hearing the grumpiness in his own voice.

"She's still resting as far as I know."

He sighed. He wasn't a big enough cad to ask his sister to make lunch for them if she needed a rest.

He hadn't made lunch for a crowd since he'd barbecued burgers for Abby's sixteenth birthday.

He hoped she'd remembered to bring hot dogs.

Shayla stared down at her paper. Drivel. She was writing complete drivel.

Her concentration had been shot from the moment she had watched him work that colt.

What an incredible thing it had been to see. The animal so wary, the man so determined, so strong, so patient.

It had been like watching a dance of sorts, a strange and fascinating dance of give and take, of power tempered with kindness.

He had held the blanket—a big, colorful thing with Navajo stripes on it—in one hand, the lead shank in the other. And he'd worked that jumpy colt from top to bottom with it, tossing it rhythmically over the young horse's back, and under his tummy, over his ears and across his tail. The horse jumped and skittered at first, and then only flinched, and then stood there quietly, with a look of placid acceptance, almost enjoyment on his face, as the blanket thumped across him.

But it was the look on the man's face that she had enjoyed the most. The look of concentration, his focus so intense, his way so sure, his eyes lit from within.

He was doing something very physical, but it was like the set of his mind shimmered in the air, and she became convinced it was that, that calmed the colt.

And she became convinced, from watching him work the horse, that she knew something of his heart.

A strong heart. And bold. But kind, too. And open.

She had seen that again when he had asked her to sing to the mare—he was willing to go beyond the boundaries of his own knowledge and experience to find the key that would unlock one more wild heart to him.

Singing to the mare had been an exquisite experience for Shayla, filling her with the oddest sense of peace, of being connected with this land of swaying grass and rising dust, with the soothing September sun and the immense blue sky, with the very breath that came out the horse's nose.

And then they had walked back to the house together, and her senses remained heightened. She was so aware of the shade of blue in his eyes, the aroma of horses and leather that clung to him, the length and strength of his stride, that she almost tingled with it, and yearned to be yet closer to him.

Shocking yearnings. To lay her head on his chest. To taste his lips. To feel the strength in those arms as they encircled her.

Even the children running ahead in the sunshine shouting and laughing were part of her strong feeling of awareness.

For a moment time stood still, and it seemed like she had everything she had ever wanted. More than she had ever wanted.

A strange feeling. Since really she was walking along with only the air that she breathed.

Somehow it made all the difference that he breathed the same air.

And then sitting in here, pretending to work, listening to his deep voice on the phone, eavesdropping shamelessly on the way he handled people. Liking it, how he talked with calm and authority, liking the way he got things done.

Feeling inordinately pleased that Nick and Maria were together, and that he hadn't been able to find them.

She snuck a paper out from behind the one with Poppy Pumpkin Seed on it. It read:

Love at first sight,
Montana skies,
Love at first sight,
Midnight eyes.
Why didn't I know my heart was breaking?
Why didn't I know it was loneliness aching?
Why didn't I run as soon as I saw you?
Why didn't I go before I found out every nuance
of blue?

She looked up suddenly, aware she was being watched. He was standing in the door, his hands hooked in his jeans pockets, smiling.

"What?" she asked.

"You sure lose yourself in that, don't you?"

She looked guiltily at what she had lost herself in. Montana skies. She looked at what she was going to lose herself in. Midnight eyes.

"Have you been standing there long?" she asked sheepishly.

"A minute or two. Are you going to read me what you wrote?"

"No!" she said, far too vehemently, slipping the paper back behind the others.

He laughed. "Shy Shayla."

Nicky darted in and landed on her lap, crumpling her work. The Halloween song had now been crumpled and uncrumpled so often it didn't matter.

"Unc Turner made lunch." He gave her a big kiss on the cheek, jumped back up and ran into the kitchen. "Wieners!" he yelled.

"What?" she said again, when Turner continued to stand there watching her, his eyes dark with amusement.

He looked at her cheek.

She rubbed it.

"Lunch," he said, his voice a thick growl. "Danielle," he called spinning on his heel, turning abruptly away from her, "go get your mom."

But his own wish to kiss her cheek shimmered in the air just as surely as his thoughts did when he worked with those colts.

In a few minutes they were once again all seated around the table, like a big family.

Shayla had never been part of a big family. It had been her and her Mom for as long as she could remember.

As a child, and maybe even later than that, she had always vowed she would have a big family. And a husband and a father for her children. Perhaps more than anything else she had missed that growing up. A daddy.

If she married Barry, she reflected, there would be no large family. He didn't like kids.

Enjoy this, she ordered herself. It might be the closest you ever come.

And enjoy it she did. A lot. Kids laughing and playing. Abby teasing her brother about the hot dogs burned black on the barbecue.

Shayla noticed he had cut some of his horse's apples and carrots into big clumsy chunks for the kids.

It endeared him to her.

"Can I name your next horses, Uncle Turner?" Danielle asked.

"Sure, sweetheart."

"Good. I hope there's lots."

"I've got six more coming in at the end of this month, so start thinking now."

"I'm going to call one Priscilla," Danielle decided.

Turner groaned and then quickly cleared his throat to hide his dismay.

"And Candyland, I'll name one. My favorite game."

"I hate that game," Turner said. "You held me hostage with that game all New Year's Eve last year."

But Shayla noticed he didn't say he hated the name, even though it was obvious to her that he did.

"And that's all for now," Danielle told him. "I'll let you know the rest later."

"Thank you," he said solemnly.

"It would be more fun to name a horse to keep than ones you train for other people. If you could name a horse, Shayla, what would you call it?"

"Something beautiful like Wind Dancer."

Lots of the horses he worked with had registered names like that or worse.

He was a man who considered himself without poetry, so it shocked him when he heard himself saying, "That's what I'm going to call the Appy mare."

She looked at him and then smiled as if he'd given her the sun—shimmering, golden, wrapped with a bow.

A stupid name for a horse, he decided too late. Too hard to say. Too many syllables.

He also knew he'd never change it now.

Abby was looking at him oddly. He returned her gaze defiantly.

The phone, thankfully, rang before he had to back down from the unsettling, knowing look in her eyes.

He got up to answer it.

"Maria," he said with surprise. "Of course he's here. He's fine. He's a fine boy, Maria. Shayla is here, too. Ten days? But—"

He stared at the phone in his hand. It had gone dead. Had she hung up on purpose, or had the line gone down? Telephone service was unreliable out here. The wind, storms, even birds, wreaked havoc on the lines.

He turned back to the table.

"That was Maria. She says 'Hi, Nicky.'"

Shayla and Abby were staring at him.

"And?" Abby probed.

"Ten days," he said, like a man in shock. "She's not coming for ten days."

Abby smiled dreamily.

"I can't stay ten days," Shayla said uneasily. "Of course I can't."

"Why not?" Abby asked. "You can work from here."

"Well, my deadline..."

"I have a fax machine," Abby said.

"It just wouldn't be right."

He couldn't help but notice she was looking everywhere but at him.

Scared to death of that little something that was leaping in the air between them. Well, he was scared to death, too. Too scared to invite her to stay. But not scared enough to tell her to go.

"I've got people picking up those colts at the end of the month," he said. "I can't be training colts and kids, too."

Whatever tension that had been in the room broke suddenly. Abby and Shayla laughed as though he'd won first prize at the Improv.

"If that was an invitation, Turner," Abby told him, "it was a darn poor one."

He glared at his sister.

She didn't look away.

"Shayla, stay until Maria and Nick come." He recognized it sounded like an order, and he was trying to turn over a new leaf. "Please?"

Say no, she told herself. Run. Get while the getting is good.

How could she say no to him when that "please" sounded like it had cost him the earth?

She looked at him.

And knew she wasn't going anywhere.

Except into the uncharted area around her heart.

Chapter Six

The house was finally quiet. Danielle and Nicky were both in sleeping bags on the guest room floor. They'd giggled long into the night, while Turner thought enviously of the bed they had both scorned.

Feeling like a delinquent Santa Claus, he got up and pulled the old saddle blanket out from under the bed.

He looked at it and hesitated. What was the big deal, really? Why did this feel like it had everything to do with his heart and not that much to do with the monk's-chamber plainness of his walls?

Annoyed with himself, he took the blanket and the same pins she had used and tacked the thing to the wall.

He climbed back into bed. It groaned a loud protest. Maybe tomorrow, if the weather held, he would set up the tent in the yard for the kids to sleep in. Danielle loved camping. Maybe he could sleep in it,

too. Even the ground had to be better than this con-
traption.

He looked at the wall across from him and scowled.

Unless he was mistaken, his snowshoes, which
he'd dumped on the floor of the back porch months
ago, were now hanging crisscrossed on the wall.

And she was staying ten days! He'd probably come
in one of those days and find the walls painted pink
and little lace doilies all over the place.

Tonight his sister, who had yet to mention when
she was leaving, had made roast beef for dinner.

And out of nothing—flour and eggs—Shayla had
made fluffy, puffy muffin things she called Yorkshire
puddings.

The kids had devoured them while he did his
darnedest to be more circumspect. But he was a man
who'd been surviving on canned stew and TV dinners, and he might have lost control a bit.

Which about summed up the way he was feeling
about his entire life.

The fact of the matter was Shayla could make pizza
and Yorkshire pudding, and she was staying ten days.

If there was anything else up her little menu sleeve
she would probably own his soul by then.

Tomorrow they were going riding together.

Since he'd been riding all his life, he didn't think
that butterfly-in-his-stomach feeling had much to do
with the horses.

A spring poked him in the back.

He tried to remember if he had ever been more
miserable in his entire life.

Over breakfast, the kids decided to be donkeys instead of pigs. He ate homemade flapjacks drowned in

pure maple syrup to the sound of braying and hee-hawing and laughing.

Shayla had her hair pulled back in a cute little ponytail. She looked about sweet sixteen, which was about the same age he had been the last time he felt so nervous about a date.

Not that it was a date, he told himself firmly. Where had that foolish little word even come from? They were going for a horseback ride.

Alone. Together. He was going to have to think of things to say.

Just like a bloody date.

"You know, Abby, I don't know if it's a good idea for Shayla and me to go. You look like you could have those babies any second."

Abby gave him a look that made him feel as transparent as a schoolboy.

"Don't be an idiot," she told him bluntly.

Danielle and Nicky cackled while he glared at her.

Then she had the gall to rub salt into the wound.

"When did that horse blanket go back up on the wall?"

He scraped back his chair.

Abby looked at him with fiendish directness. "It looks great. Did you put it back up?"

"No...Santa Claus," he snapped, which the kids thought was outrageously funny. "If you're coming," he snapped at Shayla, "come."

Let his nosy sister try and read a little romance into that.

"I think I'll stay," Shayla said. "I don't want to leave Abby with this mess."

Good. He'd succeeded in scaring her.

But Abby was having none of it. "Out," she said to Shayla. "I'm a pregnant woman. Anyone who would turn down an opportunity to ride in order to clean up a mess is an idiot, and my tolerance for idiots is way down." She softened the comment with a wink.

Still, Shayla practically ran out the door after him.

"Abby's always been like that," he said, finding enough decency in himself to shorten his stride and wait for her. "Rude and bossy. Wants everything her own way all the time."

"That wouldn't happen to run in the family, would it?" she asked innocently.

He shot her a black look that made her laugh.

Unless he was mistaken, she wasn't the least bit afraid of him.

The morning was beautiful in a way that could soften even the blackest of moods, the light clear and pure and golden.

"We're not riding those horses you were working with yesterday, are we?" she asked nervously.

Ah, fear. An emotion he could use to put himself solidly back in the driver's seat. To chase her back up toward that house before things got even more out of control than they were already.

But he didn't.

"No, none of them are far enough along to ride yet. My personal saddle horses are pastured over here." They walked to the gate, and he whistled for his horses. They had been down in the hollow by the water, and the three of them thundered over the rise toward them.

"Oh," Shayla breathed beside him, "what a beautiful sight."

He glanced sideways at her. Her face was rapt, her eyes shining, her mouth slightly open.

A fairly beautiful sight herself.

"This is Stan," he said introducing her to his twelve-year-old quarter horse gelding, as he slid a halter over his nose, and buckled it behind his ears.

"Stan? What kind of name is that for a horse?" She wrinkled her nose. It made him realize she had a really cute nose. Tiny like a button sewn on a rag doll.

"A good, solid, sensible one!" he said.

"I think he looks more like a warrior."

"Is that a fact?"

In ten days, every horse on the place would probably have exotic, goofy names.

"Wind Warrior, to go with Wind Dancer."

With a heartfelt sigh, he handed her Stan's lead. He caught the second horse.

"And this was my mom's horse. She turned twenty-three this year."

"Isn't that awfully old for a horse?"

"It's getting up there, though with what we're learning about exercise and nutrition, we're starting to see horses live into their late twenties more frequently. I kind of hope she lives forever." He was surprised as soon as the words were out, and cleared his throat. "Anyway, this horse is one hundred percent a lady, and you'll have no difficulty handling her."

"And her name?" Shayla asked.

He smiled. Come to think of it, his mom had favored fanciful names, too.

"Mom called her Lonesome Angel."

"Lonesome Angel," Shayla repeated with pleasure.

"I just call her Angie. If you'll lead her, I'll take him. Just go to one side of her and leave a little droop on the rope, don't hold her up too tight."

He watched for a moment and was satisfied. Shayla had a relaxed way with the horse. Horses were about the closest thing to psychic as he had ever seen, and even a quiet old gal like Angie would react to tense handling.

He tied Stan the Warrior to the hitching post, and then went to Shayla and untied the nice neat bow she had made in the rope.

"I always tie a quick-release knot." He tied the knot, tugged on it to demonstrate its strength and then, with a flick of his wrist, tugged the loose end and the knot dissolved.

"Why do you do that?"

Her interest was unfeigned, and he found himself explaining the knot to her and then letting her try it.

"Oh!" she said. "I'm all thumbs. Watching me do this you probably would not believe I scored quite high on my IQ test."

But she wouldn't give up, and he liked that in her. On her fifth try, with her tongue sticking between her teeth in concentration, she finally succeeded at it.

She threw her arms in the air and called "Ta-da" as if she had just tied a calf's legs in record time.

She was the same with everything else. She had to have all the grooming equipment explained to her, why it was used and what it did. And she had to do all Angie's grooming herself.

He found himself enjoying her questions, her enthusiasm, her ability to laugh at her mistakes and keep trying, and her real desire to learn.

He also didn't mind the way she looked, bent unselfconsciously over Angie's hoof with the hoof pick in her hand.

It occurred to him she was one of those people who put her whole heart and soul into things.

When she finally gave up, gasping, and set the hoof down, her face was flushed, and some of her hair had fallen out of the ponytail. There was a big streak of dirt across the front of her white shirt.

She could have posed for a picture. Rancher's wife.

He cursed himself, every bit the idiot his sister had called him, and probably then some.

He finished the feet for her, even though she protested.

She stood close as he threw the first thin wool blanket on Angie.

"See? Way up the withers, like this. Then you can pull it back, leaving the coat smooth underneath."

She smelled bewitching. She moved even closer, touching him, stretching up with the saddle pad, and dropping it over the blanket. "Like that?"

It was her hair that smelled so good. His throat felt dry.

She stepped back.

"Yeah," he said gruffly. "Just like that." *Now go stand over there—way over there—before my control is stretched beyond the breaking point.*

But instead of saying that, iron man that he was,

he tortured himself further by letting her help with the saddle, by standing way too close to her and guiding her through tightening the cinch and doing that final knot.

She did not have an aptitude for knots.

But when she finally figured it out she gave him a smile that melted a knot or two somewhere deep within him.

Suddenly he felt very glad for today.

"I want to try it once more," Shayla said, "just to make sure I've got it." It was really his fault her concentration was so terrible, she thought. The delicious aroma of him was making her head swim.

She got it backward. Again! "Damn! Sorry."

Amusement leaped in those eyes, midnight dark under the brim of his cowboy hat. "You're not writing lines for Poppy right now. It's okay. I've heard that word before."

He hadn't shaved this morning, and the whiskers were dark on the hollows of his cheek. He was absolutely gorgeous. Vital, strong, a hint of mystery about him.

She was practically shaking from being in such close proximity with him. The only knot that she'd tied with any success was the big one in her tummy.

"Here, watch."

He stepped in very close to her. He smelled heavenly, of soap and sunshine, and more faintly of leather.

There was such easy strength in everything he did—strong, weathered fingers doing things with ease that she found incredibly difficult.

She liked the way his hands moved, with the sureness of having done something so often it was second nature.

She shivered inwardly, thinking of his hands, hands that could stroke and stoke a woman to a near frenzy.

"Gone somewhere?" he asked in her ear.

His breath was warm and sensuous.

"Daydreaming," she said. "A bad habit of mine."

"A dangerous one around horses."

And around certain men.

"Okay," he said, "now the fun part."

Her eyes trailed mutinously to his lips.

"You want to ride, don't you?"

"Of course," she stammered. "It's just it was all fun."

Whether it would have been quite so much spine-tingling fun without him in such close proximity she couldn't say.

He smiled. "Just between you, me and that fence post, I think it's all fun, too. I'm horse crazy. I like all of it. Even mucking stalls. How much riding have you done?"

"Not much. I can probably manage the basics, but nothing more."

"Well, climb up and let's have a look."

She put her foot in the stirrup, stretching way up and feeling clumsy as could be. Somehow she got about halfway up and stalled, and then to her mixed horror and delight felt an iron-strong hand plant itself firmly on her rear end and hoist her into the saddle.

She wasn't quite sure whether to thank him or slap him. The look on his face would probably tell her which was more appropriate.

She glanced at him.

His face was set in solemn lines, and if there was a suspicious glitter in his eyes the shadow of the cowboy hat made it hard to see.

"I haven't done this in a long time."

"You did fine. Okay, take her out at a walk."

She did. As soon as the horse moved, she felt some fine tension in her relax, felt herself melt into the comforting rocking rhythm of the horse.

"Trot."

She nudged the horse, dredged through her memory for some faraway riding lesson and rode out the trot.

"If you're ready, lope a big circle around me."

She did, suddenly feeling freer than she had felt in years—wonderful, soaring.

She tugged the horse to a gentle stop.

He mounted his own horse in one graceful, easy swing.

"You're not bad at all," he told her. "High praise from an old cowboy. Most people have a tendency to say they're much better with horses than they really are. You have a good seat."

She could feel the heat moving up her cheeks.

"It means the way you sit the horse. But the other one's not bad, either."

So, slap him, she thought.

But she didn't. She laughed, and he did, too. They walked the horses up the road, past the house. Abby waved from the laundry line.

He cursed under his breath, and Shayla took a closer look at what Abby was hanging out.

His skivvies, in a nice, neat white row.

Nicky and Danielle rode their stick horses out of

the yard, alongside the real horses, and then Turner sent them back with promises they would get a turn to ride soon.

They went down the long twisting drive Shayla had driven in on. It seemed like a long time ago.

And then, in a place he must have had marked in his mind, he turned off and headed into the open grasslands.

He sat beautifully on his horse, straight backed but relaxed, like he'd been born to ride, which he probably had been.

"I can picture you on some snorting, wild-eyed stallion," she told him.

"Like in the movies?"

"Exactly."

"Rear up and race off?"

"That's it!"

"I don't want a horse that behaves like that. Occasionally I'll get a buck or two out of a green horse, but if I'm getting more than that, I'll go back to my round pen and do some more basics. I want the horse under me to be calm and responsive. Just like this old guy."

"So how do you make them like him? Tell me. From start to finish."

He glanced at her to see if she was serious. She was, and he saw it, and she felt a strange ripple of satisfaction that already he could read her, as though he'd known her for a very long time. So, he told her how he took a colt from being wild to finished.

"Heck," he said with a slow smile that was so unconsciously sensual it made her toes curl, "I bet I've near bored you to death."

And before she could protest that he hadn't, that she had never been less bored, he led her on a long fast gallop through the tall grass and then slowed to an easy lope.

They rode up little bluffs and through coulees, once scaring up a pair of mule deer in front of them. They halted and watched the deer bounding away. It occurred to her she felt the best she had in a long, long time. Maybe the best ever.

"That's better," he said looking at her.

"What is?"

"Your cheeks are all rosy. You don't get outside much, do you?"

"Not nearly enough," she admitted, though she wasn't sure if it was the great outdoors bringing the roses to her cheeks. "My job keeps me inside, plugging away at the piano."

"Tell me about it."

She scanned his face to see if he was kidding. He wasn't. He was looking at her intently, really wanting to hear about her job.

The horses walked side by side, and she told him about her life in Portland, and surprised herself by being able to articulate each of her dissatisfactions with writing the "Poppy Pepperseed Show."

He listened and interrupted only once, to point out a golden eagle circling lazily above them.

"Oh," she said, "I've bored you half to death." And then with a wonderful boldness born of this day, she grinned and nudged her horse ahead of his. "Catch me," she called.

They raced again, up a rise and over it, and of course, he could have caught her, but he only kept her pace, staying a little over her right shoulder and behind her, letting her find her own way through this country that was his.

His in more than the sense of ownership. His to his soul.

They had topped a ridge, and it seemed she could see forever. She slowed, and he rode up beside her.

"I talked too much," she said.

"No, you didn't. You didn't say nearly enough."

"I feel comfortable with you, more comfortable than I do with people I've known a whole lot longer."

"I'm glad," he said simply. "Tell me more."

She laughed, for the first time self-conscious. "There is no more."

"Sure there is. You never told me any of your favorite things."

"This," she said, patting the horse's damp neck and nodding at the horizon.

"And what else? Before this?"

Had there been life before this? She dredged her memory. "Hot showers on cold mornings," she decided. "And that nice clean feeling after I floss my teeth. Oh! And new socks."

He was staring at her incredulously. "New socks? You know most girls would say diamonds, or a trip to Hawaii."

"Oh," she said, flustered. "I didn't know you meant big things."

"Okay, I meant big things."

"All right then. Johann Pachelbel!"

"Boyfriend?"

She laughed at the faintly sinister tone that crept into his voice and darkened his eyes. "Not unless I'm older than I look. He composed music in the 1700s. My favorite piece of music is by him. It's called 'The Canon.'"

"But you do have a boyfriend, don't you?"

He said that as though her enjoyment of flossing her teeth would make her somehow irresistible to the male populace. As if he didn't believe she couldn't have a boyfriend.

"Kind of," she admitted reluctantly.

"Kind of? It's sort of a yes-or-no question."

How could she answer yes? When Barry didn't make her feel like this? So incredibly alive. So open to the whole world. So full of hope and wonder.

So aware of his lips and eyes and the play of his muscle underneath his shirt.

So turned on by the way his hands rested on the saddle horn or adjusted a rein or tipped his hat back off his eyes.

"He's just a friend," she said. And suddenly she knew it was true. If she had not come here, one day Barry might have been something else, one day she might have been worn down by what her mother wanted for her. But now that would never happen.

"If he's just a friend, it would be all right if I did this." His voice was deep and as sensuous as silk against heated skin.

He brought his horse in very close to hers. His thigh brushed against hers.

"What's th-that?" she stammered.

His eyes rested on her eyes and then drifted down to her lips.

"Yes," she whispered.

He leaned forward. His lips brushed hers.

The world spun beneath her. Everything changed in that moment. She knew nothing was ever going to be the same again.

She pulled away from him and touched her lips in wonder.

He smiled.

She didn't smile back. She knew nothing about him, really. But now was a good place to start.

"Tell me," she whispered, "all about your favorite things."

He backed the horse away from her and spun him on his back legs, flinging open his arm to the whole world. "This," he said simply.

A good horse. A good day. Sending her a challenging look he galloped away from her.

Hours later her legs were raw. Her muscles were screaming. Her nose was sunburned. The ponytail had long since fallen out of her hair.

And she didn't care. She could have ridden with him forever. Over the bluffs and through the coulees. Looking down from high ridges at the abandoned homesteads that spoke of a country too hard for most men.

He'd brought water, but not anything to eat, and finally near starvation, they headed back to his house.

They came in the door breathless with laughter.

Abby had made cookies in a big way. They sat down and wolfed them down for lunch, ignoring Abby's attempts to get them to eat something healthy.

Ignoring the look of sunny happiness on Abby's face every time she looked at them.

Turner took turns throwing Nicky and Danielle up in the air and catching them.

The house rocked with their laughter.

And then the phone rang.

"Shayla, it's for you."

She frowned. How could it possibly be for her? No one knew where she was. She had deliberately not given her mother the number. Maria, perhaps?

"Barry!" she said with surprise.

It seemed to her the laughter died instantly.

"How did you get this number? What do you mean from my mother? I didn't—she has what? Oh. A machine that tells her who has called? Prints the number right across a screen for her? Terrific."

She watched as Turner lay on his back in the middle of the kitchen floor tossing the kids. Why had she thought he had stopped? They were howling louder than ever. He didn't look at her.

"What is that godawful noise?" Barry asked.

"Turner is throwing Nicky up in the air."

"I hope he throws up on him."

He already has. "What a terrible thing to wish on a complete stranger."

"Your mother said he's handsome."

"I never said that!"

"Well, is he?"

She looked at him, still lying on the floor, wrestling now, Danielle and Nicky all over him.

"Yes," she whispered, then added hastily, "I mean if you like the type."

"What type is that?"

"Oh, you know. Rugged. Outdoorish." The kind they write novels about.

Abby gave her a smile as she went by with yet another tray of cookies warm out of the oven.

Shayla grabbed one and nibbled it nervously.

"Not musical or creative in any way?" Barry guessed, his voice smug with satisfaction.

"No," she agreed, "not like that at all."

"So, when are you coming home?"

Home. Her snug little apartment full of creative and musical things.

"In a few days."

"That's fairly vague."

"All right. In ten days. I'm coming…back…in ten days." Why did the word home stick in her throat?

She loved her little apartment. But if home was where the heart was, she had left hers out in the middle of the prairie.

"Ten days." A long pause. "Ha-ha, always joking, Shayla."

Turner seemed to realize he might be making it difficult for her to have a conversation and, tucking a kid under each arm, he slipped out the back door.

"I'm not joking." She felt the loss of Turner once he left the room. "Barry, I have to go now."

"I forbid you to stay there." His voice had a funny little squeak in it.

"Pardon?" she asked, shocked.

"Okay, *forbid* was the wrong word. I just wanted you to know, in the strongest possible terms, I don't want you there."

"You don't have any right to tell me where you want me."

"This is like talking to a stranger," he said coldly. "We're practically engaged, Shayla."

"Uh, no, we're not." Don't burn your bridges because of a gallop in the sun and a stolen kiss, she warned herself. ''We'll talk when I get back.''

Maybe she would get back there and just turn into the Shayla she had always been. Pliable. Sweet. A listener.

''I have to go,'' she said desperately.

''No. Your mom wants to talk to you.''

She smashed down the phone. She was surprised to find herself shaking.

Abby gave her a sympathetic look and another cookie.

The phone started to ring. Shayla stared at it.

''Don't answer that, whatever you do,'' she warned Abby, and then went out the door.

Turner was setting up a tent with the kids. ''Shayla, grab that guy wire there and help Nicky pull.''

The shaking stopped. ''Just a sec.''

She walked over to her car and opened the door. She sifted through her tapes and found ''The Canon.'' She put it in her stereo and turned it up full.

She went and took ahold of the guy rope, but lost her grip on it and tumbled over backward, Nicky on top of her.

Turner came over, that lopsided, rare grin that was his and his alone playing across the sensuous curve of his lips.

''Are you okay?''

She nodded, but he could tell she was shaken, though he suspected it was from her phone call more than her fall.

It had been a mistake to kiss her, he thought. She had a sort of boyfriend who she was still sorting things out with.

Though her face hadn't exactly lit up when she talked to him.

The way it lit up after he'd kissed her.

It had been a mistake to kiss her, for more reasons than that, though. A man would have trouble forgetting a kiss like that. It would hover there, never far from his mind, for ten days.

A sweet kiss, full of inexperience and innocence.

A kiss from the kind of girl who had all kinds of passion in her, just waiting to be discovered.

A girl who was so unaware of that side of her nature she didn't even have sexy underwear, he told himself with a rueful shake of his head. Who thought flossing her teeth was one of life's pleasures.

A simple girl. A girl like that was a forever kind of girl.

It was just like that renegade, spotted horse out there. Once you started something, you had to finish it, to see it through to the end.

To see it through to the end with Shayla, to follow that kiss any further, could well mean chaos in his life forever. Not just ten days.

Not exactly the plan he had for himself, though he was having a little trouble thinking what plan he did have for himself at the moment.

If he was smart he'd go and get on old Stan and stay on him. The Big Open, as this part of Montana was referred to, was pretty good country for a man to lose himself in for a couple of days.

Ten to be exact.

But he had horses to train, and a nephew to get to know and a sister who might need him at any minute.

It had always come down to that for him. Responsibilities.

But looking at her, he suddenly wasn't sure if it would be more irresponsible to go or to stay.

The music on her car stereo was washing over him. It was beautiful. Sad, somehow, and yet had a thread of pure hope and wonder running through it.

"You want to sleep in a tent tonight?" he asked her.

The trouble melted from her eyes. "Isn't it going to be cold?"

He certainly hoped so.

"I've got pretty good sleeping bags."

"Shayla camp with Nicky and Danielle. And Uncle Turner."

Her eyes were very expressive. She was at war with herself, just as much as he was.

And unless he missed his guess, just like him she had just lost the battle.

"Sure, I'll sleep in the tent tonight."

"Oh, goody," Danielle said. "First we're going to have marshmallows around the campfire Uncle Turner is going to build for us. And then we're going to sing. And then we get to sleep in the tent!"

He could catch his horse and ride away any old time he wanted to, he told himself.

"What's for supper tonight?" Danielle asked.

"I think I saw your mommy making lasagna," Shayla answered, regarding the tent solemnly.

He decided he didn't want to. Ride away. Not right this second, anyway.

"Lasagna isn't camping food," Danielle protested. "Uncle Turner, don't you have any canned stew?"

"No," he lied.

Chapter Seven

Shayla forced herself to finish the Halloween songs before joining everyone at the campfire.

A bonfire, really—a huge, crackling thing, set up in the fire pit on the scrubby lawn outside his living room window.

Abby came in to get another bag of marshmallows. "Those kids are going to be sick," she said cheerfully. "Not a single cookie left, and now marshmallows by the bag. Guess who the biggest offender is?"

"He ate all the cookies, too!"

"He's out there accusing Nicky!"

Shayla laughed. "Where on earth did he get the wood? There's not much around here."

"Oh, Danielle loves campfires, so Turner gets in his truck and drives two hundred miles to go cut wood for her. Foolishness." She sent Shayla a seemingly casual look.

A small thing, really, that showed a heart as big as

Montana hiding behind the stern impassive lines of that handsome face. It made tears smart behind Shayla's eyes.

"Are you coming out soon?" Abby asked.

"As soon as I'm done."

"I can't wait to hear them. Your songs."

Shayla groaned. "They're awful. The worst I've ever done. I'm probably going to be fired."

"Oh, I doubt that," Abby said. "Don't be too long. Nicky's got about fifteen minutes left in him before he turns into the monster from the green lagoon."

"I'll be right there."

In fact, she had just finished the Halloween songs, but it was another song that haunted her, running through her head again and again. She knew she would not have peace until she wrote it down.

She took out her secret piece of paper and smoothed it. She read what she had so far, and then she added:

I should never have stayed to taste the first kiss,
Then there would have been so much less to miss,
When the other life calls me away,
I'll think of Montana skies, midnight eyes and today.

She looked at it, shook her head at her own foolish whimsy and then tucked the piece of paper back behind the others.

She grabbed her jacket, stuffed the music in the pocket and went outside. Everyone cheered. As if she belonged. As if things had not been quite right without her out here.

When had she ever belonged anywhere?

Turner patted the empty lawn chair beside him, and she went and sat down. The fire crackled warmly, and stars as brilliant as she had ever seen winked in the huge Montana sky above her.

"Thank God, you're here," he murmured. "Danielle was threatening to teach Nicky 'Ninety-Nine Bottles of Beer on the Wall.'"

"He would torture us for weeks," Shayla agreed, with mock terror. "Possibly months."

"You underestimate my nephew. He would use such a weapon until at least his eighteenth birthday."

"Don't whisper," Danielle admonished them. "It's not nice."

"It certainly isn't," Turner said, lowering his brows sternly at Shayla.

"Is there a secret?" Danielle asked.

"Yeah. A secret song."

Shayla felt her heart miss a beat. Could he know? Could it have fallen out of her notebook?

But it was pure coincidence.

"She's going to sing it now, aren't you, Shayla?" Turner asked smoothly.

His eyes by firelight and starlight could inspire a thousand secret songs, she thought weakly.

"Oh, yes, sing your Halloween songs," Danielle insisted.

"Nicky be cowboy for Halloween," Nicky announced, sliding Turner an admiring look. "Shayla sing *now*."

So she sang.

The kids were wild for the songs. Shayla sang each song seven or eight times before they were satisfied.

And then it was bedtime.

She looked at that tent. What had made her agree to stay in it? Under the same roof with Turner. With no walls between them. No doors. What on earth did a man like that sleep in?

She hustled Nicky into the house and helped him into his pajamas. The top half was missing, and she found it under the bed—along with Ralph.

''Do you want Ralph?'' she said, suddenly realizing that the knit dinosaur had not been Nicky's constant companion for some time.

''No. Nicky have real friends now.''

She tried to gather him close for a hug, but he was having none of it. He squirmed free and ran out the door.

''Brush your teeth,'' she called after him.

It left her to ponder her own bedtime garb. She had a nightie, but she suddenly hated it. Flannel with a high collar, a lace ribbon at the throat, elastics around the wrist. Something like a turn-of-the-century librarian would wear to bed.

She didn't know if the oversize sweats she chose were any better.

Reluctantly she went outside. The night air was very cool now.

She slipped inside the tent.

Turner was there, in a pair of sweats and a navy blue National Finals Rodeo T-shirt, dimly illuminated by a flashlight beam.

She wondered if he was aware how handsome he was, and knew suddenly, *handsome* would be a quality without value to him. It wouldn't help him train horses. What value would it have when he rode alone?

"Nicky sleep here," Nicky said officiously. "Danielle right here and Shayla right here."

"Surrounded by your favorite girls," Turner said, but obliged him by putting the foamies where he asked and unrolling the sleeping bags. "Where do I get to sleep?"

"There," Nicky said, placing his uncle well outside his circle and close to the tent door.

"Why?"

"Bears eat you."

"There are no bears around here. Besides, I thought you liked me now."

"Nicky like you," Nicky said with surprise, as if selecting Turner to be eaten by a bear had relatively little to do with liking and disliking.

Shayla was aware of them tucking the two children in just like a mommy and daddy.

It made her feel a stab of yearning so strong it nearly took her breath away.

Her eyes met his when the children were tucked in.

She wanted him to offer to tuck her in, too.

She wanted him to kiss her again.

She wanted to move her sleeping bag over by his and sleep in the circle of his warmth.

She saw no answering desire in his eyes.

"Good night," she said awkwardly.

He turned off the flashlight and plunged them into darkness.

"Good night," he said.

She thought she wouldn't be able to sleep. Most of

her life she'd had trouble sleeping. Things got into her head and they came out to torment her at night.

But since she'd arrived here, she slept like a rock. And today the horseback ride, the hard push to get the songs done, an hour under that star-studded sky, had worn her right out. She closed her eyes. She listened to Nicky's deeply contented breathing, and over the tart smell of the tent canvas and the rubbery odor of the foamies, she could smell him. Leather and soap. And then she knew no more....

Hell's bells, Turner thought, folding his arms behind his head and staring at the tent ceiling. Had this been his stupid idea?

He'd gone from the frying pan into the fire. Not that the ground was any more uncomfortable than his sofa bed.

It was her, right over there, keeping him awake. The thought of the look on her face when she rode today, her expression of pure joy, the taste of her lips, the smell of her hair.

Even though the tent smelled the way tents that had been stored too long did, the scent of her hair still tickled his nostrils and teased his senses.

If he didn't get some sleep soon, he was going to need a helper to carry the bags under his eyes.

Only a few days ago he'd slept like a baby.

His whole damn life he'd gone to bed and gone to sleep.

I wish, he thought grumpily, they'd all just go away.

The next morning he was awakened by Nicky and Danielle jumping up and down on his stomach.

Shayla's sleeping bag was empty.

When he staggered into the house, the coffee was already on, and Shayla and Abby were at the table.

"Didn't you sleep well?" Abby asked, studying him with interest.

"I slept great," he growled. "Never better."

She shrugged, but she looked smug as hell.

"Turner, Shayla has to fax her songs today, so I'm going to take her and the kids over to my place. I'd like Nicky to meet his Uncle Peter. I think we'll stay overnight. Maybe even longer. Is that okay with you?"

As if it wouldn't be!

"Sure," he said nonchalantly, only half listening as Abby talked about taking Shayla's car and leaving the motor home.

His own bed tonight.

Quiet. Calm. A chance to catch up on his work with the colts.

Why was the foremost thought in his mind *Be careful what you wish for?*

Abby and Peter's house was beautiful, a rambling ranch with lots of stonework and hardwood.

Abby's husband was a shy, good-looking guy who obviously adored his wife and his daughter.

"Turner gave us the house for a wedding present," Abby said. "It was our family home when we were growing up, but when Peter and I got married, he insisted we take it. He said it was too big for him, and eventually he'd probably give in to the temptation of turning half of it into a stable. That's about all the convincing I needed. He's still partners with us in the ranch, but he likes those darn horses. More than people, sometimes.''

''You can control horses,'' Shayla said softly.

Abby looked at her shrewdly. ''You've got his number, I think. The question is—''

Whatever the question was, it was going to have to wait, because Danielle and Nicky started hollering about going horseback riding with Peter.

The question was, of course, Shayla thought, Could she handle it?

And she didn't know the answer, nor did she have to know, since Turner seemed to have lost any romantic interest in her after their one and only kiss.

She thought dreamily of that brief moment when his lips had touched hers yesterday, then gave herself a mental shake.

''The fax machine?'' she called after Abby.

''Second door on the right, down the hall.''

The room was a ranch office, and Shayla found the fax machine, dialed the station number and ran her papers through.

She sat there for a moment, waiting to see if there was any response.

Like, ''What is this crap?'' Or worse.

Her boss may produce a children's show, but she could swear like a trooper, and she didn't hesitate to do so when she was displeased.

Instead, what came back was, ''Shayla, fabulous work, the best you've ever done! Next: friendship gone wrong and then right again. Bye.'' Signed by her boss.

Shayla stared at the note coming over the fax and felt like her world was tilting.

She didn't even know what was good or bad any-more. Was the quality she had worked so hard to put in every song really not appreciated by anyone but herself? Would they really rather have dashed-off drivel?

Or maybe it was something else. Maybe the feeling that had gotten inside her, of being free, joined to the sky and the earth, maybe those feelings had gotten into the songs.

Maybe the way she had felt when she'd ridden be-side him, and after his lips had touched hers like a gentle welcome home after a sojourn in the desert—maybe those things had gone into the songs and made them as light and soaring as her spirits had been yes-terday.

"Something wrong?" Abby asked when Shayla found her way down to the huge, bright kitchen.

"No," Shayla said. "What a beautiful home you have."

"It's gorgeous, isn't it? My dad built it. He had a real gift. Turner has the same gift, not that you'd know it from where he's living. When he was a boy he was always drawing blueprints and houses. We all thought he'd become an architect someday."

"Did he want that?" Shayla asked, surprised. It was hard to imagine Turner as anything but what he was. He seemed a man so ideally suited to his rugged life-style. It was nearly impossible to picture him in a suit.

"Oh, I think so. Sit down. I'm making tea. The doctor said to try not to drink coffee. When my par-ents died, the ranch finances turned out to be in kind of rough shape. This is hard, hard country. Sometimes it's called The Big Open, and sometimes The Big Dry. A few years of *too* dry and things can get pretty desperate.''

''That must have been so hard,'' Shayla said sadly, ''losing both your parents at the same time and when you were all so young. How old were you?''

''I was ten, Nick was eleven and Turner was seventeen. It was devastating for all of us, and at the time, of course, I thought nobody could hurt as bad as me, but in retrospect, it was hardest on Turner. I watched him go from a fun-loving, devil-may-care boy to a stern and strong man literally overnight.

''You've got to give it to him. He turned the place around. Nick and I both had the opportunity he missed to go to college.

''But he paid a price. He seemed to forget how to laugh somewhere along the way, how to dream.'' Abby finished, looking troubled for a moment. Then she turned and poured water in the teapot, brought it over and sat down across from Shayla.

''I can't tell you the good it did my heart to hear him laughing with you and Nicky.'' She grinned. ''I don't suppose you're an angel, are you, like in that TV show?''

''I hardly ever watch TV, so I don't know the show, but me, an angel? I don't think so!'' Shayla said, smiling at the whimsy of it.

''Well,'' Abby said, ''don't be so sure. Sometimes I think we're all angels, here to help one another. Now, tell me how they liked your songs. You looked kind of stunned when you first came in. Don't tell me they fired you, after all!''

"No, not at all. The very opposite, in fact. They really liked those songs."

"Of course they did! They were wonderful songs. You saw how the kids reacted to them."

Shayla sighed.

"The weight of the world on your shoulders? Look, the tea's ready. In a teapot, not a cooking pot. I hate Turner's kitchen. It's about as homey as an army barracks, and it is impossible to cook with one pot and one frying pan."

"You did just fine," Shayla said, resisting the impulse to discuss Turner's every little domestic habit.

"Practice," Abby said with a sniff. "And a well-stocked motor home. I think visiting Turner is one step down from going camping with our motor home."

Shayla said nothing. The truth was she was rather taken with Turner's simple life-style. Barry liked toys. His kitchen had a food processor and a waffle maker and an espresso machine and just about every other appliance known to man. He had a little computer screen mounted right under one of the kitchen cabinets. He proudly possessed a stereo the size of her car, a monster TV set, a computer that could whistle "Dixie" and play Bobby-Fischer-level chess at the same time. It was much easier to see who a man was when he was not hiding behind a mountain of gadgets and gimmicks.

"There's that weight-of-the-world look again."

Shayla sipped her tea, which was delicious, and resisted the sudden, almost overwhelming, impulse to confide in Abby about Barry.

"It's not the weight of the world exactly," she

said. "It's just that next week's deadline is already looming large, and I have to think of fabulous and funny things to say about friendship gone wrong and then right again."

"For you, I bet that's a cinch."

Shayla suddenly realized she felt very comfortable with Abby and very close to her, too. Almost as though they were sisters.

"It's not difficult. It's just that it's starting to feel like I've done it all before. I could dig up old songs I've done and pass them in, and no one would ever know the difference."

"You would know the difference," Abby said with conviction.

"Oh, I know. It's all over me, isn't it? Miss Priss?"

"Shayla! Don't put yourself down for having that wonderful quality of integrity. There's not enough of it in the world. It's one of the things I find very similar about you and Turner."

Don't you dare beg to hear what the other things are, Shayla commanded herself.

"He doesn't watch much TV, either," Abby said mischievously, linking them together in one more way.

Shayla decided to change the subject, and quickly, too.

"In a few more weeks I'll have to start Thanksgiving songs," she said mournfully, feeling like a tap inside her had turned on and it wasn't going to be able to turn off. She had bared her soul like this to Turner yesterday, too.

Never once like this to Barry, or her mother.

"My world's topsy-turvy," she muttered, "and I don't want to write about turkeys!"

"Did you ever think about writing different kinds of songs, Shayla?"

"Oh," she said, "I don't really have time."

But was it the time element, she asked herself, or was it the confidence element? Scared to try something new, scared to pull out of her comfy little rut?

"I've never known a songwriter before, but I think you're very talented."

The way she spoke about knowing a songwriter, as if it was a great honor, made Shayla feel warm and teary inside.

Another unfortunate development since she had arrived in this big-sky country. Emotions that had been comfortably frozen for quite some time seemed to be unfreezing.

"You could write anything you wanted," Abby said. "You should try it."

It occurred to Shayla she was not accustomed to praise. Her mother thought her music was something she was going to play with until the right husband came along. Shayla suspected Barry saw her music only as it pertained to showcasing his own abilities.

"Maybe I will," she said with sudden defiance, her mind drifting to that snippet of a song she had guiltily penned yesterday.

"Thatta girl," Abby said. She suddenly pressed her back and closed her eyes.

"What?" Shayla asked with concern.

"Nothing," Abby said with a tired smile. "All the weight out front is pulling my back out. The same thing happened with Danielle."

"Can I do something for you?"

"Yeah," Abby said. "You can fall in love with my brother." And then she laughed. "Just kidding."

But Shayla was not at all sure she was just kidding. Or at all sure she was not already halfway there.

Silence, Turner thought, walking into the house. What a wonderful thing.

He whistled happily. The sound echoed back to him and didn't sound happy at all.

He was dead tired. He'd worked with those colts all day. He opened his cupboard and looked at his rows and rows of canned goods.

And then he scoured the fridge in search of a leftover.

He thought of pizza and cookies, and his mouth watered.

Well, damn. No way he was going to be held hostage to pizza and cookies.

It was a sad fact about horses—they could be tamed because they became hopelessly addicted to oats in very short order. Wave a bucket of oats at them, and they kissed freedom goodbye without a thought, beggared themselves completely for the contents of a bucket.

And damned if he was going to be that way for pizza and cookies. There was probably nothing to making them. Nothing. He could learn, and then he wouldn't need anybody for anything. Ever again.

Two hours later he was trying to choke down pizza that tasted like charcoal and seaweed mixed together. His kitchen looked like it could be fixed with a fire hose dragged in and turned on full blast.

He got up and tugged his hat on. He'd head to Jordan and eat there.

It wasn't until he pulled out of the drive that he realized he was making an escape from his own house.

And not the mess in the kitchen, either, but the silence.

"Get a grip, Turner," he told himself.

If he'd been hoping for company other than his own, he was disappointed. There wasn't a soul in the café in Jordan. Ma Baker wasn't even working her regular shift. The teenage girl who served him was cheerful enough, but obviously very interested in her ongoing conversation with her boyfriend on the phone. He ate like a man possessed and didn't linger.

And got home to the ringing phone.

Once when his phone rang, he could have predicted with reasonable accuracy it was Abby. Now it could be Maria. Or Nick. Or it could be Shayla's boyfriend, or her mother, or even her.

He snatched up the phone.

"Nicky here *now*."

"Hi, big guy," he said trying to ignore the warmth that spread through his chest at the sound of that gruff little voice.

"Phone to say nighty-night."

"To me?" he asked, astounded. Ah, come on. The kid was probably going to ask him to put Ralph on the line. He'd noticed the dinosaur's head poking out from under the bed in that empty guest room earlier in the day.

"You," Nicky insisted. "Nighty-night, Uncle Turner."

"Night-night, Nicky," he managed to say through a lump in his throat about the size of the World Trade Center.

The phone went dead in his hand.

"You're pathetic," he said out loud to himself. He hadn't bawled his eyes out since he was eight and had lost the mutton-busting competition at his first rodeo.

Not even when his mom and dad had died.

It would be silly to start now. Over nothing. He marched down the hall to his bedroom, took off his clothes and slipped naked between the sheets.

The freedom to sleep naked. To talk to himself.

The sheets smelled of her hair. He burrowed his nose into his pillow.

"Pathetic," he muttered again.

His big bed, where he had longed to be. Not a sound in the house.

When morning came he felt like he hadn't slept a wink.

He wondered when they were coming back.

He wondered if he was ever going to get a decent night's sleep again.

Chapter Eight

Turner sat at his kitchen table. His head felt like he had butted heads with Brahma bulls all day and belted back beer all night. His coffee tasted like crap. And his breakfast of choice, cereal and milk, had begun by tasting like sawdust and graduated to tasting like soggy sawdust.

For some reason it occurred to him his house was too small. If he had a larger house, when company arrived he could keep his own bed. He would never have to move out, never mind move back. He would never have to discover again that a certain brand of shampoo could torment a man into the wee hours of morning.

Abby had been trying to tell him for some time that his house was too small.

Really, it wouldn't take that much to knock out a wall and add on a few feet of living space. He made a rough sketch on a paper napkin.

For what reason? his mind asked him.

He crumpled up the napkin. Who knew for what reason? Did a man have to have a reason? All right, here was a reason. He hadn't had a good sleep for days. Nights. He was losing his mind.

The phone rang.

He exercised willpower. He took another long sip of his tar-flavored coffee and watched the phone, let it ring another ring. No sense having anyone think he was just hanging by the phone waiting for it to ring like someone pathetic and desperate and lonely.

On the fourth ring he moseyed over and picked it up.

Abby. Not Shayla. If he liked his life so predictable what was that little worm of disappointment in his belly?

"Turner, we're going to stay here a bit longer. You don't mind, do you?"

His sister actually wanted him to *beg* her to bring Shayla back. He could hear it in her voice.

"Why would I mind?" he snapped. He ordered himself not to ask how much longer. "How much longer?" he asked.

"Tonight, anyway. Guess what happened?"

"I give."

"Henry offered to give her a plane ride."

"You keep her away from him!" He sensed himself falling into a trap. With big steel teeth.

"What? Why?"

Oh, she could sound so innocent when she set her mind to it. She actually wanted him to say he was jealous. He could hear it in her voice.

Was there a delicate way to tell his sister that her

neighbor, one of his rodeo buddies from a way back, was a womanizing cad?

If there was, it completely escaped him. "Henry Smith is a horny SOB."

Shocked silence. He had finally managed to shock his sister.

Nope. Wrong again. She was laughing. She'd trapped him into saying that. Now she'd think he cared.

"Nicky and Danielle are going along. As chaperons. Are you happy now?"

What exactly did he think the shame in caring was?

"No!" he snapped. "I'm not."

"You're grumpy as a bear this morning, Turner. I'm glad I'm not there."

"Me, too," he shouted, and hung up.

And then he smiled. And then he laughed. His sister had just succeeded in making him lose control.

And what exactly was the shame about that?

Maybe it was about damned time.

He went and uncrumpled the napkin. Drew a few swift lines.

There. A new bedroom. Presto. Enough room to accommodate two or three visitors.

Leave it, Turner, he ordered himself.

But the addition of a bedroom had left him feeling strangely dissatisfied.

If a man was going to settle down, which of course he wasn't, but if he was, this house could probably be made quite livable.

If he pushed out that living room wall ten or twelve feet he bet he could put a baby grand piano in it. And then if he knocked out the wall between his room and the little bedroom, his guest capacity would be back down, but the master bedroom would be big enough to include an en suite, one with a Jacuzzi tub in it.

The thought of her and him together in a Jacuzzi tub made his mouth go dry.

Her. Why was he so surprised that she showed up in the Jacuzzi? Who had he thought the baby grand piano was for? He'd played a musical instrument once. A triangle, in the grade one rhythm band. If he recalled, the teacher, an enormous fat lady with gray hair in a tidy bun, had hit him soundly on his head with her ruler for ringing it at the wrong time.

Impatient with himself, he crumpled up the napkin with unnecessary savagery and tossed it toward the garbage. It missed, and he left it on the floor, just like the good bachelor that he was.

He stomped over to the door and pulled his cowboy hat off the hook, shrugged into his jean jacket.

Shayla was wrecking everything. She wasn't even here and she was wrecking everything. Training colts required patience, control, concentration. Sleep.

But actually, once he was with the horses, he settled down just fine.

The reality check.

This was his world, plain and simple.

He couldn't be with these animals and not concentrate one hundred percent. Wasn't that the appeal of it? They required an intensity of focus that took a man right out of himself.

Brought him right into this moment of soft snorts and sweat and dust and made the rest of the world fade into nothingness.

He realized he had really started working horses after his parents died.

Letting it carry him away from the pain. When Nick had gone he had worked even harder. He didn't know whether he was running away or being healed.

And a few days ago he had never asked himself such questions.

He ignored the noise for as long as he could, but Henry's plane buzzed overhead repeatedly, making an annoying sound like a crazed bumblebee. He kept passing over, and he had the gall to wag the wing tips, as if he expected Turner to wave.

Knowing Henry, he probably had his meaty hand resting casually on Shayla's thigh. And knowing her, which he really didn't, he reminded himself grimly, she was probably too damn polite to tell him to move it.

Let them wait for him to wave. Until hell froze over.

He remembered Danielle and Nicky were up there, too. He could picture them with their noses pressed against the window, waving frantically at him. What was a man to do?

He waved.

From that distance, they would never know how grudgingly.

"Hi."

He nearly jumped out of his skin, and the colt jumped three feet sideways. He whirled.

"Sorry." Shayla smiled.

"You sneaked up on me!"

"Actually, I made quite a lot of noise. You looked very intent on what you were doing."

He realized he was still scowling. He made an effort to relax.

The plane buzzed over them. Lower. Henry trying to get a better look, Turner figured. Shayla waved.

"I thought you were up there." He gestured at the airplane. *With a hand on your thigh.*

"The kids were going to go for a ride. I hate airplanes. They make me throw up."

"Really?" He tried unsuccessfully to hide his delight.

"What are you doing?" she asked.

"This is called driving a horse between two reins."

"I remember you telling me about it yesterday, but I can't quite remember what it does. I mean, you aren't training them to pull plows are you?"

His clients, most of them into world-class reining horses, would perish at the thought.

"It starts getting them ready for neck reining. Starts to build the relationship of trust between me and him. He starts to figure out nothing I ask of him is going to hurt him. And he starts to feel mighty pleased with himself when he understands what I want."

"He looks mighty pleased with himself."

Turner glanced back at the horse, who was dozing between the lines.

"Which one is this?"

"Nicky calls him Marmalade."

"And what do you call him?"

"I'm scared to say."

"Come on."

"Shoe," he muttered.

He glanced at her. She was trying not to laugh. She looked right pretty this morning, dressed in jeans and an oversize plaid shirt, a bandanna knotted at her throat.

She smiled at him. "I like Marmalade better."

He laughed. "Me, too."

"Show me what you do."

"It's not that interesting."

"You seem to find it interesting."

How could you argue with that? He picked up the two long reins, thick cotton ropes, really, and clucked at the horse who moved obediently forward. He turned the horse right and left, was pleasantly surprised when the colt trotted on voice command, and came to a neat halt when he called out "Ho."

"I think that's interesting," she said. "He was completely wild when I first came."

"He's a sucker for oats," Turner said, attempting modesty and giving Marmalade an affectionate rub on the nose. "Quick learner, too. A good horse."

"I kind of thought—" She was suddenly shy. She looked at her sneaker.

"What?"

"If you wanted—" She was still studying that sneaker.

"What?" he asked, his heart hammering at a ridiculous rate.

"You and I could go horseback riding again. I packed a lunch at Abby's. But if you're busy, I understand."

He stared at her. She'd packed a lunch. She'd driven thirty-five minutes. She'd passed on a free airplane ride. Never mind that would have made her sick.

She wanted to be with him.

Just as much as he wanted to be with her.

And suddenly he wondered why the hell he'd been running. Why not find out if it was all in his head, or if he was going to be ordering a piano anytime in the near future? He wondered if he'd have to leave that wall out to get the piano in.

"Well," he said, "I guess if you went to all the trouble of packing a lunch."

She burst out laughing.

And he realized it was funny. A grown man acting as though he found lunch irresistible, when it was really her.

"I can't think of anything I'd like to do better than go riding with you," he said softly.

She rewarded his effort at honesty by beaming, a light coming on behind her eyes that turned them the sexiest color of green he had ever seen.

He went to her in one long stride. He lifted her chin. Her eyes were huge, and her lips soft and moist. Calling his name, begging, though she spoke not a word.

He surrendered. He surrendered control completely.

It tried to resurface. The controller in him croaked, "Maybe we're going way too fast."

The very thing he'd accused Nick of all those years ago with Maria.

How real can it be? he'd shouted. *You've known the girl about a week!*

God was having a little laugh at him now, because he'd known this woman in front of him even less than that. He counted back on his fingers mentally. Five days. And yet something in him knew, if it was ever going to be...

"Too fast?" she whispered. "I thought there were no speed limits in this state."

He kissed her then. Tasted her completely. Felt something like life begin to stir within him.

He backed up.

He was going to have to put a tight rein on that part of it. She had the right idea. Ride. Eat lunch. Get to know each other.

Fast, though.

"You can't be taking walls out in the middle of a Montana winter."

"What?" she said, baffled.

He laughed. The laughter felt wonderful inside of him, like a deep brook that had been dammed up too long and was ready to overflow its banks.

"Nothing. Let's go saddle us some horses." He held out his hand to her.

Hers slipped inside it like it had been made to fit there. Her skin was soft and silky, but her grip was strong.

That lump was back in his throat. Bigger now. Big as the whole damn city of New York.

Shayla had woken this morning in a big, beautiful four-poster bed at Abby's, and had wished herself back in a tent.

Yesterday morning she had woken up first, and been able to study him sleeping in his sleeping bag.

He was gorgeous. His face relaxed and whisker shadowed, his lips moving slightly. She'd made herself get up and go get coffee before the yearning to touch him overcame her.

Now she'd woken some twenty-odd miles away in

his sister's house, and the yearning to touch him, to be with him was just as strong. No, stronger.

She liked Abby. She adored the kids. Peter made her laugh. Handsome Henry had looked at her with an expression that really should have made her feel something other than amusement.

The truth was she didn't want to waste one minute of her time with them. She had only ten days. She wanted to ride this feeling inside her to the outer limit. To experience it totally and wholly, to not go away from here regretting what had not happened, what she had not done.

Abby and Henry had pushed for the plane ride.

"I think I'll start work on next week's songs instead," Shayla had replied without enthusiasm.

Abby had sent her one of those looks she was getting used to. A look that said, "I know something you don't."

Except that maybe Shayla did know, or was starting to.

And when Henry had gone, Abby had turned to her and said, "Why don't you go spend the day with Turner?"

"Oh!" Shayla had said, feeling the blood rush up her face in what she knew would be a most unbecoming—and telltale—shade of red. The way Abby was looking at her, that small cat-got-the-cream smile playing around her lips, Shayla felt as though her thoughts had been pulled out of her head and put on display.

"I couldn't. Possibly."

"Why not?"

Why not? "He's very busy."

"Humph."

"And it would seem very forward of me."

"Forward? You need to change your reading materials."

"And he probably wouldn't want to."

"I'll tell you something about my brother. The more he wants something, the more he appears not to. The cowboy thing. Invulnerable. It's really quite silly. It took me a long time to cure Peter of it."

Shayla remembered when she looked at Turner in the tent the other night, wanting to be close to him, seeing no answering yearning in his eyes.

His eyes. Well, yes, they'd been guarded. Something in them he didn't want her to see?

"Take a chance," Abby said with a grin. "You take life too seriously."

Shayla considered how "take a chance" was so different from what she was accustomed to hearing. Never take a chance. Never do anything out of the ordinary. Always conform. If you did something as simple as drive to Montana, you were crazy.

"He does, too," Abby mused. "Takes life too seriously. Maybe you wouldn't make such a good match. Serious each other near to death on a cold winter's night."

"A match?" Shayla squeaked. "Really, you have the wrong idea."

"I know. I was just teasing. You really do take everything far too seriously. But you know, it's not every day you're going to find yourself in Montana."

"Poor Turner, turned into my tour guide."

"Like I'll bet he really minds," Abby said dryly. She studied Shayla. "Good grief, you believe yourself. Tell you what. Make him lunch. He'll find you irresistible. A colt going after a bucket of oats.''

Shayla couldn't help but laugh. ''I guess without the lunch there wouldn't be much hope he'd want to spend the day with me.''

Abby shook her head in mock despair. ''Girl, you're working around the cowboy thing, again. You have to give him an excuse.''

Now, hours later, Shayla was so glad that for once in her life she'd said yes to an adventure. Yes to possibility. Yes to not knowing where exactly it was leading or what would happen next. For once in her life she had decided she didn't care what it looked like first. Who cared if she appeared forward?

Come to that, the man lying on the blanket beside her, with the remains of lunch littered around him, probably thought forward was just a gear on his truck.

They lay on their backs watching the sky, the grass swishing in the wind, the horses grazing contentedly.

She was so close to him, she could feel the heat coming off his body. She thought of moving a little closer but decided that was a little too forward, even for the new and bold version of her.

Shayla tried to think when she had last felt so good. So full to the top with contentment. The answer seemed to be never.

''Tell me about all those belt buckles on your dresser,'' she insisted drowsily.

''Most of them are for bull riding.''

He said that with casual dismissal, as if they'd been won doing nothing more dangerous than playing chess.

She gave in to the desire to turn her head and look at him. His profile was strong and relaxed.

She felt a little thrill of happiness that they were able to feel this comfortable together.

"Do you still do it? Ride bulls."

"Nope. Grew a brain."

She laughed, loving how every now and then he slipped into a colorful cowboy vernacular mostly for the effect. He laughed, too, knowing she was on to him.

"What was the appeal of it, anyway?"

He turned and looked at her, reached up and tangled a finger in her hair.

"I don't know for sure. I've never tried to find words for it before."

She read a lot of loneliness into that. No one to share his best moments with. And his worst. But it was the life he'd chosen, and a man like him would have had a lot of options.

"It's about being strong, somehow," he said thoughtfully. "Knowing everything your body can do. And take. It's brutal. And satisfying."

She suddenly thought of how he moved. In his own way. With an ease about his body. Confident. A man who had pitted himself against incredible odds. Raging bulls. Montana's extremes in weather. Horses who objected to being ridden.

He had taken his body to the limits and come to know exactly what it would do for him, how it would work for him.

It showed. In the way he walked, in the set of his jaw. It showed in the easy strength with which he could heft a saddle or toss a bale.

It showed in the humor and patience that burned deep in quiet eyes.

He was a man who had come to rely on his own strength. Maybe too much. Both his greatest asset and his greatest weakness.

Because could a man like this ever learn to share the load with someone else?

He was so incredibly attractive and in so many different ways. Not just physically; his spirit was a beautiful thing. Who he was showed right down to his soul. How many women had seen these same qualities in him, for who could miss them? How many had offered to walk his lonely road with him?

And yet he still walked alone.

"Maybe—" he hesitated "—maybe bull riding is about fear, too. Facing what scares you the most and not blinking."

He lifted his shoulder, as if shrugging that off.

"Did you ever get hurt?"

"Outside. Nothing serious. Bruises and abrasions. Busted my arm once."

Outside, she thought. An interesting statement. "What about inside, Turner? Did you ever get hurt inside?"

"Not by the rodeo."

"Your brother?"

"How did you know?" he asked, a touch sharply.

"It shows in your face when his name comes up. And when you look at Nicky. Plus, Abby told me you were estranged, but not why."

She had known him only a few days, but so much about him did show. Maybe especially the parts he most tried to keep hidden.

"We had a fight. My fault. Years ago."

"About Maria?"

"I thought they were too young to be so serious. He'd just finished college. He had his whole life ahead of him."

"So, how do you feel about him coming here? With Maria?"

"Men don't talk about these things. Men talk about the Super Bowl," he told her.

"Isn't that in January?"

"Okay. Beef prices. Pickup trucks."

"Thank goodness I'm not a man," she answered back.

"You're not kidding."

"So, how do you feel about your brother coming?"

"You don't look like a bulldog."

"You shouldn't let looks fool you."

He took a deep breath. "It's not just him, it's Maria, too. I owe the lady an apology about as big as Montana. So, I'm happy they're coming. And scared to death, too. More than I ever was about riding a bull."

"The scariest things are inside, aren't they?"

"So what's scary for you?"

She plucked a blade of grass and put it thoughtfully between her lips.

"It'll seem silly. To a man who rides bulls."

"Try me."

"Change. Change scares me the most."

He looked at her intently. "That doesn't sound silly at all. Change scares me nearly spitless, too."

"It does not!"

''You saw me trying to hustle that horse blanket off my wall and out of my house.''

''That wasn't about change.''

''It wasn't?''

''It was about control.''

''Same animal, Shayla. Tell me about the horse blankets in your life.''

He listened to her talk. Her very voice was like music. He could hear in her a discontentment with her job, but not with music.

He suspected that music led her to move in her own way. It was what gave her that inner stillness.

Not like Celia who had been outwardly focused.

Her world was within her.

The question was, really, could she handle his world? Oh, this ranch was the only place for him. But he'd been born to these wide-open spaces, this way of life. The remoteness, to him, was part of the appeal. He liked pitting himself against the sometimes-brutal forces of nature. He didn't mind a long haul to the nearest neighbor.

But she might see each of those things differently.

Winter was coming. And winter was bone chilling, maybe even frightening to some in its intensity.

It wasn't just a life, it was a life-style, and a hard one.

Ask her, a voice inside him prodded. After all, she's a lady who takes pleasure in simple things. New socks, for crying out loud.

But what would he really be asking?

It wouldn't be fair to pose a question that asked her to consider something he hadn't given proper thought to for a long, long time.

The future.

Besides how could she answer a question that she really knew nothing about? She might think she could handle this kind of life and then find out she couldn't.

This was the simple truth: the longer she stayed, the harder it was going to hurt him when she left.

Look that one in the face without blinking, Mac-Leod, he ordered himself.

"Let's go," he said gruffly.

She looked puzzled and hurt.

Maybe, he told himself, the time of his life when he could learn to be with another person had long since passed.

She was sensitive. Look at her gathering up her stuff, pretending she hadn't been hurt by his abruptness, when he could see the pain in the set of her shoulders and the tilt of her chin, in the color of her eyes.

How many times would he hurt her without meaning to?

The plain truth was she was probably better off with her "sort of" boyfriend.

They probably had whole worlds in common.

The silence ached between them as they rode back.

He pulled his horse to a stop on a rise along the way.

"Do you see something?" she asked.

He nodded to the east. "See that dust? Better than a doorbell."

"Maybe Abby bringing the kids back? I think she said she was going to come back this afternoon. Nicky and Danielle were wild to get back to you."

"To me?"

"Their favorite uncle."

He said nothing, but watched the dust rising in the east. Unless he was mistaken, which he was not, the dust was coming up in three separate clouds, a mile or two separating each one of them.

Three vehicles coming up the long road to his house.

He couldn't believe it. The last time there had been three vehicles on this road—he frowned—was never. There had never been three vehicles on this road. His life was turning into a three-ring circus.

It felt like it was all her fault, this lady who sat so quietly beside him, sitting that horse as if she'd been born to one.

It didn't bode at all well for his sleep.

With a sigh and the slightest pressure from his legs he sent old Stan bounding forward toward the unknown.

And she came right beside him, leaning into her horse, the wind tossing her hair, as if she would ride beside him into the unknown forever.

Forever.

Look that one in the face without blinking.

Chapter Nine

Abby had already arrived when they finished unsaddling the horses and went up to the house.

Turner thought the end of his road was beginning to resemble a parking lot. Abby's motor home. Shayla's car. His truck and now Peter's ranch truck.

He shook his head and glanced back down the road. Dust swirls still coming. He guessed one to be a mile away, the other slightly more. He went into the house right behind Shayla.

How good it felt to come home with her, even though the silence of his own making stretched between them unnaturally.

"Hi," Abby called.

Danielle and Nicky came roaring out of nowhere, and both attached themselves to his knees and cackled with laughter as he tried to disentangle himself.

He looked up to see Abby beaming and Shayla smiling.

He also saw that damned paper napkin, that he knew he had left on the floor, all smoothed out and hanging on the fridge. Hanging by a little black and white cow magnet. He didn't own any such thing.

What was his sister trying to do to him?

"Peter with you?" he asked.

"No, he had some work to do. The kids had to get back to their Uncle Turner."

"I'm not sure why," he said sourly, but when he looked down at them, each clinging to a leg with all their tiny might, he felt something soften in him.

He glanced at Shayla, and her soft smile said she knew exactly why.

"Company coming," he said crisply, easing himself over toward the fridge with his two weights still attached to his legs. It was like trying to slog his way through a swamp, and there wasn't any way to do it without attracting attention.

"Who?" Abby asked, with enough surprise to let Shayla know there wasn't much company that came down that road. He glanced at her again.

Yup. She was still looking at him, her smile turned just a touch sad. Branding him lonesome and pathetic.

"I don't know. I saw the dust." He casually reached out and scooped the napkin with his house sketch off the fridge.

Abby smiled.

He gave her an evil look and put it in his pocket.

A door slammed outside.

Abby went to the window. "It's a red Barracuda."

Turner saw Shayla pale. He pried Danielle's fingers from his leg, but by the time he'd pried Nicky loose Danielle had reattached herself.

"Enough," he said sternly. They both ignored him.

He dragged them over to the window and looked out over Abby's shoulder. A very stylish, full-figured woman was standing beside a dusty and aging sports car. She was wearing a filmy pink scarf over her hair, and funny-shaped sunglasses. A huge white Angora sweater topped tiger-striped tights.

Abby made a face at him, then returned her attention to their visitors.

A man got out the driver's side. Good-looking, almost criminally so, but soft, going pudgy around the middle.

"It's my mother, isn't it?" Shayla whispered. "Tell me it isn't."

"Your mother wouldn't wear orange-and-black-striped leotards would she?" Turner asked tentatively.

Shayla moaned. Turner slid her a look. She looked suddenly pale and tired, not at all like the vital and laughter-filled woman who had ridden beside him today.

"Who would that be with her?" he asked.

"With her?" Shayla howled. She ran to the window. "Oh, good grief. Barry. What are they doing here?"

She looked around as if she wanted a place to hide. He felt as though he'd like to do nothing better than hide her.

Sling her over his shoulder and race back down to the corral with her. Put her on a horse and head into the endless land with her.

But, of course, he couldn't do that.

The three of them stood unmoving, watching. He could hear her mother's voice. It reminded him of that grade-one teacher who'd smacked him with the ruler. Something like fingernails on a blackboard.

Where on earth had Shayla's beautiful voice come from?

"Why, isn't this the cutest little place?" she was saying shrilly in a tone that clearly indicated she thought the place was anything but cute. "Sitting out here in the middle of the windswept prairies just as cute as a bug in a rug."

He shot Shayla a look loaded with sympathy. She wouldn't look at him.

Grab her and run for your life, a voice inside him suggested.

But he was a mature adult now. He had to face unpleasantness. Unfortunately. Because unpleasant it was going to be.

The woman hadn't shut up since she got out of the car.

And now she was at his door, peering in the screen. "Haalloo," she called.

Danielle and Nicky looked at each other, giggled, released their death grips on his legs and ran away.

Smart kids.

Abby went to the door and opened it. Unless he missed his guess his sister looked strangely thrilled by this latest development.

Shayla's mother swished in the door and posed like an aging movie star, looking around, her sharp little gaze taking in everything, and finding it wanting. Especially him.

"Shayla, honey," she said. "We did find the right place!"

"What are you doing here?" Shayla asked, her face white and her tone tight.

"I was so worried about you! When I couldn't get you on the phone, I just had to come. Barry came—"

The door squeaked open and Shayla's mother turned and gave an approving smile. "Here he is now. Barry, we found the right place. Look! Here's Shayla."

Barry gave Shayla a little half wave that Turner found gratingly theatrical.

"I can't believe you did this," Shayla said to her mother, returning Barry's little wave halfheartedly. "How could you?"

Turner watched with interest as her mother's red-painted mouth formed a perfect little bow of hurt.

"You haven't even introduced us to your new friends, Shayla."

She was particularly looking at Abby's big round tummy with interest.

Grudgingly, Shayla made introductions. Turner couldn't help but notice her mother seemed disappointed that Abby was his sister and not his live-in girlfriend or the maid he'd seduced.

He might have squeezed just a touch too hard when he took Barry's hand. The pudgy hand was pulled from his, and he was treated to a wary, wounded look.

"Why are you here?" Shayla asked again.

"We came to get you!" her mother announced, as if this was a surprise that would just delight the hell out of Shayla.

Her mother's name was Esmeralda, which he was pretty sure had also been the name of his grade-one teacher. Or Esther, or Hester or Henrietta. Something like that. The kind of name a writer gave a witch.

"Essie," she insisted coyly.

"I'm not ready to go yet," Shayla said, folding her arms over her chest.

From the shocked look on Essie's face—and Barry's—Turner had a feeling Shayla hadn't stood her ground nearly enough. He felt like giving her a nice little congratulatory smack on the shoulder, but restrained himself.

"But," Essie said, "but Shayla, we've come all this way, and we've worried so much about you, and my bursitis is really bad—"

Don't buy it, he told Shayla silently.

She was looking at her mother skeptically, but with the skepticism was just a hint of guilt.

"Come, come," Abby said. "Everybody sit down. I'm going to make some coffee and some tea. We might as well all get to know each other."

He managed, just barely, to refrain from asking why on earth they would want to get to know each other.

Shayla shot Abby a look at least as black as the one he did.

She ignored them both. "You should probably stay the night," she was saying blithely. "You've had a long drive. It'll be dark soon, and these roads can be treacherous in the dark."

"Only if there's a blizzard. Uncommon for September. Even here," Turner muttered, and was ignored by everyone except Shayla who gave him a wan and grateful little smile.

"Morning," Abby said firmly, ignoring him, "is

soon enough to figure out who is going where with whom.'' She laughed. ''Did I use *whom* right?''

''As a matter of fact,'' Barry said, ''it would...''

Turner didn't listen to what he said. He didn't like the other man's voice. Smooth and greasy as axle oil. He tuned it out and stared at his sister. Overnight? And pray tell, where was he going to put everyone?

But Abby was already figuring. ''Now the kids could come in the motor home with me. Essie, you could have Turner's room, and Shayla can have the small room, and Barry could have the sofa bed.''

Barry on the sofa bed. Justice.

Abby looked at him with interest. ''Oh, and Turner.''

He smiled at her tightly.

''Well, you could have the tent, Turner.''

''Thanks,'' he said dryly. *Why was she doing this to him, and why did she have that twinkle of pure devilment in her eye?* She was thoroughly enjoying shaking up his nice, orderly world. And she wasn't even trying to hide the fact.

''I suppose I could take the tent,'' Barry said doubtfully.

''Oh, no, have the sofa bed. I insist,'' Turner said.

''Well,'' Barry said happily, ''only if you insist.''

''I do.'' He'd be willing to arm wrestle him—loser got the sofa bed. He eyed Barry's arms and felt slightly smug. No doubt who that would be.

He heard the slamming of a door and then another one. He went to the window. So did Abby.

''Oh!'' she said, and was running awkwardly for the door. ''Nicholas!''

Turner felt like he'd been slammed in the stomach. He stared out the window.

His brother was getting out of a battered old pickup. Could it possibly be the same one he'd left in, all those years ago? Nick had filled out through the chest and shoulders, but it was in his face where Turner could see the real transformation. When he'd left, Nick had been a kid. Now there was no doubting he was a man.

He watched Abby race into his arms and Nick pick her up with easy strength and whirl her around. He watched Maria hanging back, shyly, her dark eyes liquid.

He'd thought he had more time to prepare for this.

Shayla came and stood beside him. Her fingers touched his arm. "Nick?" she asked.

He nodded and looked at her. It was in her eyes how completely she understood his distress at this moment.

"It'll be okay," she said softly.

"Yeah."

He turned to see Essie looking at him with a beady-eyed look of pure suspicion. Barry had found a plate of cookies that interested him far more.

Abby must have brought fresh cookies with her. For a crowd.

He thought of that napkin, burning a hole in his jeans pocket.

Here was the truth of the matter. A renovation was not going to do the trick. Nothing short of a whole new house would accommodate all these people.

He plucked the rumpled piece of napkin out of his

pocket and tossed it carelessly in the garbage. It hit this time.

Taking a deep breath, he went out the door.

Nicky and Danielle exploded past him.

Nicky stopped in his tracks on the second stair, and then Nicholas turned, as if he were in slow motion, and stood staring at his boy.

A look Turner couldn't even describe came over Nick's face. A brilliant light seemed to suffuse it, and he dropped like a man in a trance to his knees. His arms came up.

Nicky stood frozen on the steps. For a moment he leaned into Turner's leg which was right behind him.

He looked up at Turner, his dark eyes wide. Looking for something in Turner's face.

Turner nodded.

It was all Nicky needed, confirmation from someone he had come to trust.

Turner felt honored by that trust.

Nicky exploded off the stairs, his little legs churning toward Nick.

He screeched to a stop in front of him.

"Daddy?" he whispered, his tone so full of awe and wonder that Turner's heart nearly broke in two.

And then Nicky hurled himself into his daddy's arms and cried when those arms folded around him— loud, hiccuping sobs that seemed to come all the way from his stubby little toes.

"I've never seen him cry before," Shayla said softly. She had come up beside Turner, and he'd been so engrossed in the reunion he hadn't noticed her.

"How'd he know Nick was his dad?" Turner asked softly.

"I'd like to think his heart knew."

"I'd like to think Maria had a picture of him," Turner responded, trying desperately to lighten the mood of heavy emotion.

He failed. Shayla slipped her arm through his. He could feel her shaking. He glanced at her and saw the silvery tear slip down her cheek.

"Daddy, where have you been so long?" Nicky whispered hoarsely.

Shayla wiped at the tears.

Nick stood up, the boy in his arms pulled hard into his shoulder, his eyes as wet as his son's.

And it seemed to Turner that his brother's dark eyes met his with anger and recrimination.

Most of it deserved.

"There goes the tent," Abby happily told Turner from where she was standing holding Maria's hand.

Turner looked at Maria. She was looking at him with something in her eyes he couldn't read.

He went slowly down the steps. He stopped in front of his brother.

He held out his hand and was surprised when Nick shifted his son's weight and took it.

Strength in his brother's handshake now. And in his eyes, too.

"Welcome home," Turner said softly.

"This is my uncle Turner," Nicky introduced them officiously.

Nick laughed. So did Turner.

"Your uncle Turner and I know each other," Nick said. "He's my brother."

For some reason the words struck a chord deep in Turner.

My brother. The other half of my heart. But why, when he thought of the other half of his heart, did his gaze move of its own accord to Shayla, still standing on the steps, mopping furiously at her eyes.

"Daddy, where have you been?" Nicky whispered again, touching his father's face with a sturdy little hand, as if convincing himself it was true. "Nicky needed you."

Again Turner felt it in his own heart. A sharp twist of pain and remorse.

Was there anything he could do or say now to make it right?

Maria had come up beside them. She smiled at him with a shy sweetness that held no bitterness in it.

"Hello, Turner," she said, her hand going up almost involuntarily to touch her son's back, to be a part of that circle of love.

Part of a circle of love, Turner thought almost dizzily, looking around him.

Shayla was standing on the porch. Her mother was peering out from behind the door. Danielle was jumping up and down, and Abby's eyes were starting to swell from crying. His brother and Maria and Nicky were here, real and beautiful.

It was a choice, really, to belong to a circle like this or to walk away.

A choice that meant giving certain things up.

Like control. Like calm. Like quiet.

And getting other things in exchange.

Like what was in Shayla's eyes right now. It occurred to him that now that Maria and Nick were here she had some choices to make, too. She could go home with her mother and the doughboy. If she wanted.

And she could stay.

If he asked her.

"Come on," Abby said, coming to him and putting an arm around his shoulder. "You don't have to sort out the whole world right now."

"Where I'm going to sleep tonight would be enough for me," he said gruffly. "Abby, maybe you should take them to your house. You have so much more—"

"Nonsense," she said. "This is going to be so much fun."

"You aren't looking at sleeping in the barn," he snapped.

Over coffee and cookies and noise so loud it made his head spin, he realized he needed to talk to them. To Maria and his brother. Alone if that was ever going to be possible.

"Hey, guys," Barry said, as if he was the host of this little get-together, "I brought a tape of the last show. Who wants to see it?"

Everyone had been inordinately impressed when Barry had announced with false humility that he was an actor. To Turner's annoyance everyone but him wanted to see the show.

They had to drag some kitchen chairs into the living room, but everybody managed to pile in, and Barry flipped on the VCR with easy familiarity. Turner still had to read the instruction book if he wanted to tape something.

While everyone else laughed and cheered at Barry making a big fool of himself as Bo-Bo the Clown,

Turner watched morosely and glanced as often at Shayla as he could without drawing attention to himself.

Her mother seemed to intercept every glance.

Shayla sat stiffly, between her mother and Barry, and she didn't seem to see his glances at all.

Turner forced himself to look at the screen. Bo-Bo was singing a song, dancing and bowing to Poppy Pepperseed, who was a wooden puppet in a pinafore and braids.

The song was as cute as could be. Bo-Bo was an idiot. Even with a purple-polka-dotted pair of pants on and a little red ball on his nose, it came through to Turner that Barry was self-centered and full of himself.

Turner got up. And was he so different?

He hoped to slip away unnoticed. Shayla came out of her trance, and her eyes followed him, but Barry had his flabby arm over one of her shoulders and her mother had her hand on her leg.

He went outside.

The night was clear and bright and beautiful.

He walked toward the barn.

He heard the tap of steps behind him and turned, hoping it was her.

But it wasn't.

It was Maria.

He waited until she caught up. "Thank you for bringing him home," he said quietly, "and for trusting me with your boy."

"I always trusted you, Turner."

He looked away from her. "Trust misplaced."

"I don't think so."

"Your son hasn't had a father because of me and my meddling. I need you to forgive me for sticking my nose in where it didn't belong."

"All right," she said simply. "I forgive you."

He looked at her again. She was a beautiful girl, with lovely doe-shaped eyes and an expression of such gentleness and warmth. How could he not have wanted that for his brother?

How had he managed to miss that, all those years ago? How was it he had been unable to see what was essential about her?

And why could he see it so easily now?

But he knew the answer. Because something in his own heart had thawed.

"Thank you," he said gruffly.

"It won't help one little bit until you forgive yourself."

Beautiful and clever. Maybe perceptive was a better word. A gift women had. Being able to see the thing you most wanted to keep hidden.

"Yeah, you're probably right. And that might take a while."

"Turner, I always knew you had a good heart. That you loved Nick fiercely and that you did what you thought was best for him."

"At what price to you?" he snapped. "I looked after my brother at your expense. Or thought I did."

"I'm not going to pretend the years alone were easy," she said quietly. "But when I last saw Nick he was a boy. Now he's a man. I think he has you to thank for the steel in his eyes today."

"Great," Turner growled.

She stood up on her tippy-toes and planted the most tender of kisses on his cheek.

"Why did you send Nicky here?" he asked, as she turned to leave him. "You could have just as easily sent him to Abby's."

"I wanted you to see what love could do." And she turned and ran lightly back toward the house.

What love could do, he thought sourly.

Turn a man's world upside down. Fill up his house with noisy relatives and yelling kids.

In the barn, way back under some old lumber and other junk, was an old trunk.

He dug it out and opened it.

Inside it were blueprints he used to draw when he was a boy. He unrolled one carefully. The paper was brittle and stained by dampness.

He looked at the house he had drawn once.

He could hardly believe the hand had been his. There was youth and hope in each amateurish line of the drawing.

A beautiful house with lots of windows, a prow-shaped front and a cathedral ceiling.

The house of a man who dreams ordinary dreams. Of children. Of family.

Of a mother-in-law from hell?

He shoved the drawing back in the trunk. In the morning he'd talk to Nick, and then he was getting the hell out of here. When he came back they'd probably all be gone.

And he'd be able to sleep at last.

He found a musty old bedroll back in the junk, climbed up on top of his hay supply, rolled himself up in the blanket and closed his eyes.

He supposed Shayla and Barry really had quite a lot in common. The guy could sing and dance. So what if he dressed up in a clown costume for a living? He was an artist, just like her.

They could probably be very happy together.

Besides, the dragon, Essie, seemed to like Barry. She seemed to not like Turner one little bit, if the nasty looks she had kept casting his way were any indication.

He was going to have to talk to Nick tomorrow. He didn't think Nick was going to be quite so forgiving as Maria.

Nick would probably punch him in the jaw.

He realized a good hard punch to the jaw felt like something he could handle with a lot more ease than a good hard heart-to-heart.

He cursed at the hay jabbing him in the back, rolled over and pulled out the offending stalk. He rolled back. Another had replaced it.

Through the slats in the barn he could see the house lights going off one by one.

It occurred to him he might be kidding himself.

He might well never sleep again.

Especially after she was gone. He'd be haunted by her sweetness. By the memories of her laughter and the smell of her hair.

Choices to make.

Leave.

Stay.

Love.

Or be alone.

Play it safe.

Or go dangerous?

By morning his choices seemed to have grown to monstrous proportions.

His head felt like he'd been butting it against a rhinoceros's, and belting back straight whiskey.

His brother came through the door.

"Turner?" he called into the darkness.

Turner called out "Yeah" and swung up. He groaned. "God, I feel old."

"You don't look any too young, either," his brother said with a shake of his head, coming over to him and peering at him through the morning murkiness. "I'm sure you could have slept in the motor home. It sleeps about twenty-three from what I could tell."

"Then I wouldn't have been able to feel quite as sorry for myself," Turner pointed out dryly.

Nick laughed, startled. "Are you developing a sense of humor in your old age, Turner?"

"I hope not," Turner said, but felt stung. Hadn't he always had a sense of humor?

"Abby sent me out here," Nick said uncomfortably.

"What for?"

"She said she's not feeding us until we sort it out. And Maria backed her up."

"Women," Turner said with a snort and then looked at his brother. He'd grown. Filled out physically, but there was something in his eyes now, too.

A man.

"I hate it the most when they're right," Turner said grudgingly.

"Me, too," Nick said sitting in the hay beside him.

"I'm sorry, Nick. I made some really bad moves, and I'm sorry."

"You know what Maria said to me? She said I was lucky to have a brother like you."

"Women."

"I hate it the most when they're right," Nick said quietly. "Turner, I shouldn't have needed her to tell me you took on a lot when you were too young to take it on. That you always did what you did out of love."

"I think they all watch Oprah too much," Turner said with a shake of his head.

"Watch who?"

"You've been with those grizzly bears too long."

"You're not going to like this, Turner, but I really like those grizzly bears."

"Yeah. I kind of figured."

"I'm going back. Maria and I got married. They're coming with me."

It was on the tip of his tongue to tell his brother that was no kind of life for his wife and child. He bit his tongue instead. What did he know about the kind of life a wife and child wanted or needed?

It occurred to him that what he really wanted to say was that he'd miss them. He'd like them closer. He wanted to watch his nephew grow up.

This was what love did. Put this lump in your throat the size of the whole world.

"Congratulations, Nick," he managed to say.

"We won't be strangers," Nick told him. "I want you to come visit. We'll come visit. Maria's already arranging to come back when Abby's baby is born. Turner—"

"Yeah?"

"I really missed you."

"I really missed you, too, Nick." They felt like the hardest words he had ever said. He looked at his watch. The face seemed blurry. "Ah, geez, I gotta go. Horse sale in Lewistown this morning."

"When are you going to be back?"

His brother's disappointment that he was going almost made him change his mind and stay. Almost. A man just couldn't let his heart start making his decisions for him.

Though that begged the question: What part of his body was sending him running to a horse sale in Lewistown he had decided two months ago *not* to attend?

His truck keys were hanging from a hook by the back door. Once upon a time, a long time ago, he left them in the truck.

Abby didn't think that was a good idea with the kids around.

He tried to sneak into the house. He didn't want to be interrogated by his snoopy sister right now. He certainly didn't need to start asking her permission to go to horse sales.

But only Barry was in the kitchen, munching happily on what looked to be a raspberry Danish.

"How'd you sleep?" Turner flung at him, trying to keep the malicious interest out of his voice.

"Sleep? Never better. Love that bed."

Turner looked for signs of sarcasm. The man was an actor after all. "You love that bed?" he asked, incredulously.

"Well, you know most of those sofa beds are killers."

"And that one isn't?"

"Slept great," he said again, taking a big bite out of his pastry. "Do you want one of these? I make them myself."

He wouldn't have eaten one if he was starving, which he was. Shayla deserved a man who could make pastry. Yes, she did.

Was it possible there really was nothing wrong with that bed? That all the problems he was having sleeping were in his own head?

"Quiet out here," Barry commented.

From a different part of the house he could hear Shayla's mother. Howling about something. Or maybe singing. It sounded like the death screech of a wounded turkey.

"It used to be," he said. "It used to be."

Chapter Ten

"**W**here's he going?" Shayla asked, watching from the kitchen window as Turner pulled his truck out from between her car and Peter's truck. He backed around so swiftly that for a moment she held her breath, thinking he was going to hit her mother's ridiculous red sports car. Intentionally. Instead he roared away in a cloud of dust and spitting rocks.

She turned and looked at Barry. He was making a big pile of pastries in the toaster oven he'd borrowed from Abby's motor home.

"He said something about Lewistown," Barry mumbled with a mouthful of pastry.

It registered with Shayla that it wasn't registering at all with Barry that she was interested in that cowboy.

"Who went to Lewistown?" Abby asked, coming down the hall, squeezing water from her freshly washed hair with a towel.

"Turner," Nick said, coming in the back door. "He said something about a horse sale."

"Ha. As if he doesn't have enough horses. He's doing the cowboy thing. Riding off into the sunset. Or sunrise as the case may be. Alone."

Shayla tried to appear as if she didn't care.

Her mother made her entrance, dressed in a sweater with a large sequined cat head on the front of it. The kitchen suddenly seemed so tiny and cramped Shayla wanted to scream.

What kind of person could stand a kitchen like this? Live in it day after day without even noticing?

"Shayla," her mother said, "you might as well pack your bag. You aren't needed to help look after Nicky anymore, and you and Barry and I can—"

Shayla didn't let her finish her sentence. She went out the back door and walked down to the barn and then to the paddock behind it.

No wonder he didn't care about the kitchen, she thought. With all this space out here, why did he need any in there?

Don't forgive him, she warned herself. If you forgive him for that kitchen, you'll forgive him for leaving.

He had let all the horses out in the pasture except for Wind Dancer, who was well stocked with hay and water.

Which meant he planned to be away for a while.

She heard someone come up behind her. "Go away," she said without turning around.

"It's me," Maria said.

"Oh." Shayla turned and gave her a weak grin. "I thought it was my mother."

"I know," Maria said gently, and then, "What a gorgeous horse."

"I hate this horse," Shayla said childishly. "Ugly freckled thing. Turner's one and only true love."

Maria came up beside her and rested her chin on the fence. "You like Turner?"

Shayla didn't know what to say. *Like* didn't seem strong enough.

Oh, God, it hit her why *like* didn't seem strong enough.

She loved him.

She loved that lonesome cowboy.

"It doesn't matter how I feel about him," Shayla said stiffly. "He's gone."

"It matters to me how you feel about him," Maria said quietly.

"Why is that?"

She smiled. "I could have sent Nicky to my sister's, you know. She lives right in Portland."

"What? Then why on earth did you send me halfway across the country—"

"I don't like Barry."

"Pardon?"

"I don't like Barry," Maria repeated stubbornly. "I've watched him around the pool a couple of times. He's been there when I picked up Nicky from your place. He's not for you. He's so much like your mother it's scary. Disapproving. Controlling."

"Oh, Maria. I was never going to marry Barry. I told him that."

"Your mother would have worn you down."

Shayla's own suspicion exactly.

But not now. She could never settle for anything

less than that tall, sure cowboy with the startling blue eyes that held the whole world in their depths.

"Why did you send me on this wild-goose chase?" she asked Maria querulously, trying so hard to hide her hurt. "What on earth does that have to do with Barry? And my mother?"

"Everything. You needed to get away from under their thumbs for a while. Find out who you really were."

Shayla stared at her friend, astounded. "Maria! You are every bit as controlling as them."

"But I'm the good fairy," she said with a sweet smile. "Shayla, I wanted you to see Turner."

"But why?"

"Because he's a real man. Because almost from the first minute I saw you I could picture you with him."

"You were matchmaking!" Shayla said. "You sent me here thinking I'd fall for him!"

"And didn't you?" Maria asked shrewdly.

She wanted to shout no. But her heart simply would not let her lie about this. "Yes," she said sadly. "I did. And now he's gone, and it hurts. I'll be leaving today with Barry and my mother."

"Don't you dare! I know a thing or two about these MacLeod men, Shayla. Once they've given away their hearts that's it, for life."

The mare chose that moment to charge wild-eyed at the fence, snorting angrily.

Both the women leaped back and then laughed nervously.

"That," Shayla said emphatically, "is what he has given his heart to. I wish them every happiness. I'm leaving here today. I'm leaving with Barry and my mom. I want my old life back.''

Her old life where she didn't have to feel so much. Maria looked at her sadly.

They both heard an earsplitting scream.

''That's Ma!'' Shayla exclaimed. They took off at a dead run for the house.

''She's having a baby,'' Essie was screaming. ''Oh my God, I'm going to faint. She's having a baby.''

They heard the words long before they got to the house. Shayla ran up the stairs and in the back door. If the kitchen had seemed small before, now it seemed absolutely claustrophobic with Abby sitting on a chair looking pale and in pain.

Shayla's eyes went to Abby who nodded at her with relative calm.

''Can Henry get here with his airplane?'' Shayla asked.

''I think it's too late,'' Nick said. ''Lean on me, Abby, we'll put you in Turner's room.''

''He'll like that,'' Abby said with a grin.

''My God,'' Essie was wailing, and waving the phone receiver around over her head. ''The phone's dead. How can I call 911? The phone's dead. The phone's—''

''Mrs. Morrison,'' Nick interrupted her, ''would you look after Danielle and Nicky? Maybe take them for a walk?''

Shayla could not help but see some of Turner's own strength in his brother. The take-charge attitude, the calm. He even handled her mother!

Her mother looked startled and then hung up the phone. She stopped screaming.

"Why, of course I will," Essie said bravely. "Of course I will help in any way I can. Shayla, you come with me."

"I'm staying with Abby. She might need me."

Her mother stared at her, astounded. "I really think, dear, you'd be much more help to me. You know how I am with children."

Having survived her own childhood, she did know how her mother was with children. Nicky and Danielle could probably survive a few hours with her.

"I'll come, Essie," Barry said comfortingly, sending Shayla a you-are-a-bad-girl look. "There, there, it will be all right."

Maria and Shayla exchanged glances and then went down the hall to Turner's room.

Turner had driven by the horse sale without getting out of his truck. There was a deep and gnawing restlessness in him that even a new horse was not going to solve.

If he was a drinking man he would go for a drink.

But he wasn't.

All the way to Lewistown he'd thought about her. Tracing the moment his life had gone out of control to the arrival of her little car in his driveway.

But, of course, that wasn't quite true.

If he was really honest about it, it was when Nick left, that things had started changing in him.

No.

Before that.

When his parents had died.

He had stopped feeling things.

And she had come along and made him start to feel again.

She had made him face the vast emptiness his life had become.

Really, he thought, what she deserved was a medal. Maybe that is what he would do. Buy her a nice going-away present, something that would help her remember him.

He drove slowly up Main Street, the historical charm of the sandstone buildings completely lost on him today. He tried to think what had possessed him to come here. Out of the corner of his eye he caught sight of a new storefront, nestled right in between his favorite rifle shop and Western-wear store.

Lacy Grace. He slammed on the brakes and stared at the tasteful display of lace items. Someone honked.

He found a parking spot and made his way back to the store. *This is what happens when a man doesn't get enough sleep,* he told himself grimly going in the front door.

"Give me one of everything in that front window."

Not an appropriate farewell gift, his inner voice chided him.

"That's because I'm not going to say goodbye to her."

"Sir?"

"Size eight. Or something like that."

So what if Barry could make pastries? Turner had a few talents of his own.

Suddenly a shiver moved up and down his spine. He whirled around.

He could have sworn he heard Abby call his name.

Suddenly he remembered her yesterday, pressing at

her back, saying how it hurt. Then he remembered her almost-feverish energy.

Hadn't he read somewhere that pain like that could be back labor? And that the birth of a baby could be foreshadowed by a sudden burst of energy?

"Wrap what you've got ready, quick. My sister's having a baby."

The sales clerk looked at him incredulously. Not an appropriate gift for someone having a baby.

"Just throw the damned stuff in a bag."

She handed it to him, and he flew out the door. He could feel his pulse beating in his throat.

He knew with every fiber of his being that his sister was having those baies. And it was her own damn fault he wasn't there. How could she expect him to be rational when he'd been trying to sleep on fold-out beds and in tents and on hay bales?

He stopped at the nearest pay phone. The lines were down at his place. Again. He called her home number. No answer. He got in the truck and put the pedal to the metal.

He gave the fact there were no speed limits in Montana new meaning.

He made it home in record time and ran for the door. Shayla's mother and Barry were snoozing in lawn chairs, bundled up against the fall bite in the air. Nicky played at their feet with a little dump truck.

"Hi, Uncle Turner. Want to see my truck?"

"Where's Auntie Abby?"

"Having a baby," Nicky said with disgust. "Danielle doesn't want to play with me."

Turner flew up the stairs and into his house. Danielle was at the kitchen table moving paper dolls around in a desultory fashion. She looked at him, and he saw she'd been crying.

"Mommy really hurts," she whispered.

He took a minute to bend down and touch her cheek. "Mommy's going to be just fine, Danielle."

He saw something lighten in her face and marveled that his niece trusted him so implicitly.

He was not a praying man, but Abby shrieked as he went down the hall.

"God," he said. "I gave that little girl my word. Don't let me be wrong. I'll do anything."

"I'm so glad you're here," Shayla breathed when he burst through the door. He squeezed her hand. Aw, what the hell? He kissed her on the mouth.

Nick looked up at him. "Just in time, big brother."

He went over to Abby. She was sweating and panting but obviously not too alarmed by the whole process. She held out her hand to him. He took it.

She was glad he was here, too. He wondered what he had done in his life to inspire people to trust him like this, to care about him, to feel an ease when he was present?

He didn't know what he had done, but he felt both humbled and grateful.

"Do you feel them, Turner?" Abby asked raggedly.

"The pains?" he asked, startled.

"No, silly. Mom and Dad."

He shot his brother a startled look, raised his eyebrows. Nick shrugged.

"I feel them," she said. "Right here in this room."

For a panicked moment he wondered if she was dying.

"Here it comes," Maria said breathlessly. "The head is out! Now the shoulders! It's a boy!"

The room was filled with a stunned silence. And then the baby began to wail. He was a tiny little thing. Turner would have been amazed if he hadn't known there was another one on the way.

They were all laughing and crying, when suddenly Abby groaned. "Oh, God, here comes number two!"

The second baby, as wrinkled, red and beautiful as the first, was a girl.

A few minutes later the babies were snuggled on their mom, tears of joy and weariness coursing down her cheeks.

"I told you they were here," Abby croaked to her brothers, tears running in rivers down her face. "I'm calling these babies Winston and Sarah after Mom and Dad, our own special angels, who brought us all back together, who went to so much trouble to get Shayla here..."

Her voice drifted; she closed her eyes in contentment.

"Do you know what she's talking about?" Nick whispered.

"I told you she watches too much Oprah," Turner said gruffly, but he did know exactly what she was talking about.

Destiny.

Angels making sure that everything turned out okay, even when men used every ounce of their iron to try and wrest a little control over a situation.

"Danielle," he called down the hall. "Come on in here and meet your new brother and sister."

Danielle came. "Is Mommy all right?"

"I'm just fine, sweetheart. Come here."

Danielle went and sat gingerly on the edge of the bed. "Oooh," she said looking at the babies.

"Nick, why don't you and Maria go get Peter?" Turner suggested. He turned to his sister. She looked wretched and beautiful all at the same time. He leaned over and smoothed the sweat-dampened hair from her face and peered into those tiny wrinkled faces.

"Thanks a lot," he growled at her. "More people to find beds for."

"Turner," she said huskily, "you're never going to be able to renovate this place to accommodate a half-decent-sized family."

"Aw, hell, I know it," he told her.

She laughed huskily. "I just need to sleep for a little while. Could you all just leave me for a bit?"

"You're incredible," he told her.

She reached up and touched his cheek, ever so gently. "So are you. Go on, now."

They moved into the kitchen.

He looked at the heaps of cookies everywhere. Abby's burst of energy must have really been something, to keep Barry from even making a dent in these cookies.

He went to Shayla.

She looked up at him with shining eyes.

"Nicky," Maria called, and went out the back door looking for her son.

A moment later they heard Essie shrieking. "I lost him! But I just went to sleep for a minute. Oh, my God, I lost the little boy! Oh, God!"

"Mother-in-law from hell," Turner muttered, and then felt a shiver go up and down his spine. He hoped

Nicky hadn't decided to feed the horses on his own today. Then he remembered the boy's fondness for Wind Dancer.

Before he could think twice, he was running toward the paddock, Shayla right behind him. Just beside her ran Maria and Nick and behind them, waddling so fast it would have been laughable under other circumstances, were Essie and Barry.

Turner slowed when he could see inside the paddock, not wanting to startle Wind Dancer.

The little boy was standing right in the middle of the enclosure holding out a few strands of grass in his hand.

Turner stopped and held up his hand to the stampede of people behind him. "This horse is not used to people," he said with grim authority. "Please stay back. And," he added sternly in the direction of Shayla's mother, "be quiet."

She shut her mouth with an indignant snap.

Turner faced Shayla. "I want you to sing, and keep moving slowly toward Nicky. No fast moves. Be calm. She's not going to hurt him. Or you. Stay calm."

Shayla nodded, her eyes large and full of trust for him.

What had he ever done to deserve that?

If he wasn't careful he'd be hearing the swish of angels' wings just like his sister.

"I'd do anything to be the one going in there," he told Shayla, "but sometimes a nervous horse will tolerate a woman or a child approaching it, but not a man. Don't ask me why."

He thought he knew why, though. The horse, that

most telepathic of animals, sensed in women and children the softness, the lack of threat.

"Go," he said. She slipped through the fence, and then with her shoulders back, took a small step forward and began to sing.

It was not one of her Poppy songs but a song he had never heard before, the melody so sweet and haunting it sent tingles up and down his spine.

Love at first sight,
Montana skies,
Love at first sight,
Midnight eyes.

Wind Dancer, who had been eyeing Nicky with wary unease, and who was squashed back into the far corner of her pen, pricked up her ears.

"Good girl, Shayla," he called. "Keep singing. Nicky, don't move."

Shayla sent him a look over her shoulder. He saw the courage in that look and was awed by it.

He thought of his sister having those babies and knew men had a great deal to learn from women about the true nature of courage.

Her voice rose up, strong and free, soaring, with a little hint of sadness running all the way through it.

Why didn't I know my heart was breaking?
Why didn't I know it was loneliness aching?
Why didn't I run as soon as I saw you?
Why didn't I go before I found out every nuance
of blue?

Shayla eased forward, and the mare blew out her nose and shook her head but made no move toward the woman or the boy.

Love at first sight,
Vast, empty land,
Love at first sight,
Work-roughened hands.

She was almost at Nicky now, easing forward with calm. The mare took a hesitant step forward, but there was no aggression in it. Suddenly Turner realized Shayla was singing about *him*.

I should never have stayed to taste the first kiss,
Then there would have been so much less to miss,
When the other life calls me away,
I'll think of Montana skies, midnight eyes, and today.

She reached Nicky, who looked up at her with the most beautiful smile, at least as mesmerized by her song as the horse was.

"Take his hand and back out slowly," Turner called to her. "Don't turn your back on the horse, and don't run."

Shayla didn't back out, but stood holding Nicky's hand and looking at the mare. She sang.

Love at first sight,
Haunts forever,
Love at first sight,

I'll never forget.

Never.

The last note hung in the air, and the mare walked slowly toward them.

Shayla held out her hand.

Wind Dancer came and stood before her, dropped her head and gave Nicky a little sniff.

The little boy reached up and touched her. And then Shayla touched her, too.

Wind Dancer stiffened for a moment, and then all the stiffness seemed to dissolve from her.

"I'll do anything," Turner had promised God, not an hour ago.

And already his debt was being called in.

Love.

Love her with his whole heart and soul.

Turner ducked through the fence and went slowly toward them. He could hear Nicky talking to the mare in his gruff little voice.

"Don't be so mad," he told the horse. "Love will fix it."

Shayla knew Turner was coming because of the way the mare's attention shifted slightly away from her. She waited for the horse to bolt away, but she didn't, not even when Turner was standing right beside Shayla, shoulder to shoulder.

She glanced up at him.

And was almost blinded by what she was in his eyes.

Of course, the words *mother-in-law from hell* that he had muttered in her mother's direction had been going through her brain for some time now.

Why would he be thinking of *her* mother in those terms?

Slowly Turner ducked down and scooped up Nicky. The mare surprised them all by nuzzling him softly.

"Love really will fix it, won't it?" he said softly. "I can see you riding this horse, Shayla, as clearly as if you were doing it right now."

"Me?" Shayla said, astounded.

"She's yours, you know. She has been from the first moment you sang to her."

"Mine?" Shayla said, turning and stroking the horse with exquisite and tender hands.

He was calling her mother "mother-in-law" and giving her his most precious possession.

It could only mean one thing.

Couldn't it?

"You want to marry me, don't you?" she whispered.

"I was thinking you'd never ask," he said with a smile that lit his eyes and lit her heart.

"You're supposed to ask!" she told him, the laughter bubbling in her like it would never stop.

It occurred to her it was never going to stop. This feeling of joy. Of utter completion that she felt in his company.

"Okay," he said. "Will you marry me, Shayla? Will you share my life with me and fill it with music and laughter and children?"

"And don't forget the mother-in-law from hell," she reminded him.

"How could I?" He kissed her soundly, right in

front of them all. "Now go home, everyone," he called, "the show is over."

Maria laughed. "This is one show that has just begun."

Shayla turned to try and soften the blow for her mother. For Barry.

He was chewing complacently on a cookie. Not the least heartbroken.

And her mother was looking at Barry with a strange little light gleaming in her eye.

"Is your mother about to corrupt a younger man?" Turner whispered.

"I think so."

"I hope it keeps her busy for a good long time."

"Me, too."

They turned and walked out of the corral, the horse shuffling along behind them like a favored family pet.

As they walked up the worn path toward his house, Turner talked.

"So," he said, "there will be you and me and some kids eventually, and Abby and her brood, and Nicky coming to visit...." He glared in the direction of the house. "I think I'll just tear it down and start again."

"We don't have to worry about that right now."

He looked at her. She didn't care about the house. As they approached his truck, he realized she probably didn't care about all that lace and froth in the cab, either.

She cared about him.

The look in her eyes set something inside him free. Some closely held tension eased and uncoiled, and in its place something warm came. And filled him. Healed his heart and his soul.

"What are you smiling like that for?" she asked.

"Because I love you. And because I have a funny feeling I'm going to get the best sleep of my entire life tonight."

"Oh!" She stopped and peered thoughtfully in the window of his pickup truck.

He looked over her shoulder.

Little scraps of delectable lace underthings had scattered everywhere on that wild push for home.

She smiled at him, a smile full of mischief, a hint of passion dancing in eyes gone gold.

"You're going to get the best sleep of your life tonight, Turner? I kind of doubt that."

* * * * *

MORE MacGREGORS ARE COMING!

In November 1998, *New York Times* bestselling author

NORA ROBERTS

Brings you...

THE MacGREGOR GROOMS

Daniel MacGregor will stop at nothing to see his three determinedly single grandsons married—he'll tempt them all the way to the altar.

Coming soon in Silhouette Special Edition:

March 1999:
THE PERFECT NEIGHBOR
(SE#1232)

Also, watch for the MacGregor stories where it all began!

December 1998: THE MacGREGORS: Serena—Caine
February 1999: THE MacGREGORS: Alan—Grant
April 1999: THE MacGREGORS: Daniel—Ian

Available at your favorite retail outlet, only from

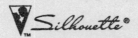

Take 2 bestselling love stories FREE

Plus get a FREE surprise gift!

Special Limited-Time Offer

Mail to Silhouette Reader Service™

3010 Walden Avenue
P.O. Box 1867
Buffalo, N.Y. 14240-1867

YES! Please send me 2 free Silhouette Romance™ novels and my free surprise gift. Then send me 6 brand-new novels every month, which I will receive months before they appear in bookstores. Bill me at the low price of $2.90 each plus 25¢ delivery and applicable sales tax, if any.* That's the complete price, and a saving of over 10% off the cover prices—quite a bargain! I understand that accepting the books and gift places me under no obligation ever to buy any books. I can always return a shipment and cancel at any time. Even if I never buy another book from Silhouette, the 2 free books and the surprise gift are mine to keep forever.

215 SEN CH7S

Name	(PLEASE PRINT)	
Address	Apt. No.	
City	State	Zip

This offer is limited to one order per household and not valid to present Silhouette Romance™ subscribers. *Terms and prices are subject to change without notice. Sales tax applicable in N.Y.

USROM-98   ©1990 Harlequin Enterprises Limited

HE CAN CHANGE A DIAPER IN THREE SECONDS FLAT BUT CHANGING HIS MIND ABOUT MARRIAGE MIGHT TAKE SOME DOING! HE'S ONE OF OUR

July 1998
ONE MAN'S PROMISE by Diana Whitney (SR#1307)
He promised to be the best dad possible for his daughter. Yet when successful architect Richard Matthews meets C. J. Moray, he wants to make another promise—this time to a wife.

September 1998
THE COWBOY, THE BABY AND THE BRIDE-TO-BE
by Cara Colter (SR#1319)
Trouble, thought Turner MacLeod when Shayla Morrison showed up at his ranch with his baby nephew in her arms. Could he take the chance of trusting his heart with this shy beauty?

November 1998
ARE YOU MY DADDY? by Leanna Wilson (SR#1331)
She hated cowboys, but Marty Thomas was willing to do anything to help her son get his memory back—even pretend sexy cowboy Joe Rawlins was his father. Problem was, Joe thought he might like this to be a permanent position.

Available at your favorite retail outlet, only from

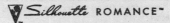 **ROMANCE™**

SRFFJ-N

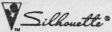

COMING NEXT MONTH

#1324 THE NINE-MONTH BRIDE—Judy Christenberry
Virgin Brides

It was supposed to be a marriage with just one objective—to make a baby! Or so Lucas Boyd and Susannah Langston thought. But the more time Susannah spent in Lucas's arms, the more he hoped to convince her that the real purpose was...love.

#1325 WEDDING DAY BABY—Moyra Tarling

They'd shared one passionate night eight months ago. But now naval officer Dylan O'Connor had no memory of that night—and Maggie Fairchild had an all-too-apparent reminder. Could Maggie rekindle their love before the stork arrived?

#1326 LOVE, HONOR AND A PREGNANT BRIDE
—Karen Rose Smith
Do You Take This Stranger?

Penniless and pregnant, young Mariah Roswell had come to rancher Jud Whitmore with the news of his impending fatherhood. But would the man who'd lovingly taken her virginity take her into his heart and make her his true-love bride?

#1327 COWBOY DAD—Robin Nicholas
Men!

Pregnant single mom Hannah Reese had learned the hard way that not all cowboys lived up to a code. Then she met rodeo star Devin Bartlett. Rough, rugged, reliable, he made her feel...and dream...again. Could *he* be the perfect cowboy dad—and husband?

#1328 ONE PLUS ONE MAKES MARRIAGE—Marie Ferrarella
Like Mother/Like Daughter

Gruff Lancelot Reed never thought he'd love again—until Melanie McCloud came crashing into his life. Lance wanted to have nothing in common with this spirited woman, but the intense attraction he felt for her was more than even he could deny....

#1329 THE MILLIONAIRE MEETS HIS MATCH
—Patricia Seeley
Women To Watch

Millionaire Gabe Preston didn't know what to think of beautiful Cass Appleton when she landed on his property, searching for her missing cat. But as the fur flew between them, Gabe started hoping he could help her find something else—love.